THE DOUBLE

MARIA TAKOLANDER was born in Melbourne in 1973. A senior lecturer in literary studies and creative writing at Deakin University in Geelong, Victoria, she is the author of a work of literary criticism, *Catching Butterflies*, and the poetry collections *Ghostly Subjects* and *The End of the World* (forthcoming). Her poems have featured in annual best-of anthologies for the past seven years. This is her first book of fiction.

THE
MARIA
(AND OTHER STORIES)
DOUBLE
TAKOLANDER

TEXT PUBLISHING MELBOURNE AUSTRALIA

textpublishing.com.au
The Text Publishing Company
Swann House
22 William Street
Melbourne Victoria 3000
Australia

First published in 2013 by The Text Publishing Company

Cover and page design by WH Chong
Typeset by J&M Typesetting

Printed in Australia by Griffin Press, an Accredited ISO AS/NZS 14001:2004 Environmental Management System printer

National Library of Australia Cataloguing-in-Publication entry
ISBN: 9781922079763 (pbk)
ISBN: 9781921961946 (ebook)
Author: Takolander, Maria, 1973–
Title: The double (and other stories) / Maria Takolander.
Dewey Number: A823.3

This book is printed on paper certified against the Forest Stewardship Council® Standards. Griffin Press holds FSC chain-of-custody certification SGS-COC-005088. FSC promotes environmentally responsible, socially beneficial and economically viable management of the world's forests.

This project has been assisted by the Commonwealth Government through the Australia Council, its arts funding and advisory body.

CONTENTS

I

The Red Wheelbarrow
5

Three Sisters
29

The Double
47

The Obscene Bird of Night
79

Mad Love
91

Paradise Lost
117

The Interpretation of Dreams
133

The War of the Worlds
175

II

A Roānkin Philosophy of Poetry
199

Roānkin and the Judge of the Poetry Competition
211

Roānkin and the Research Assistant
225

Roānkin and the Librarian
241

'Or shall I pretend it's not me but somebody else strikingly like me, and look as if nothing's the matter?'

FYODOR DOSTOYEVSKY, *The Double*

I

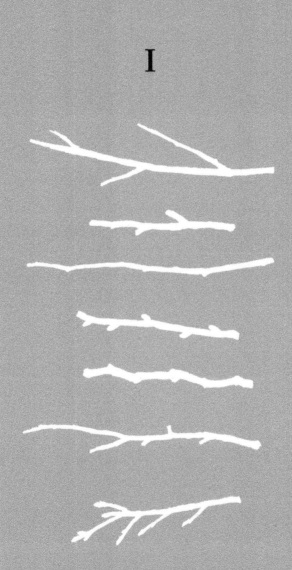

The Red Wheelbarrow

I HEARD a growl, deep and low, and then a yelp. I had been lying awake in the dark—I always tried to stay awake when Dad was drunk and angry—and when I heard the noise I got out of bed, crossed the hallway and pushed open my parents' bedroom door. It was after midnight, but the light was on, and the room looked as if it was shining.

Mum and Dad were sitting up in bed, the dark veneer of the bed head framing them from above the waist and the white sheet messed up around their legs. Dad's mouth was smeared with blood. It was on his teeth. He was panting. Mum was looking into her lap, where she was squeezing her left fist with her right hand. I could

see the thumb sticking out, flesh hanging off and blood streaming down.

I helped Mum out of bed. 'What do you think you're doing?' Dad said, still sitting on the bed in his T-shirt and jocks. His words were slurred, and I could see that he was having trouble focusing. I led Mum down the hallway and into the bathroom, switched on the light, and closed the door behind us.

Mum wouldn't let me drive her to the hospital. 'It isn't so bad this time,' she said in her accented English. She sat on the edge of the bathtub in her short nightie, swaying and crying a little, clutching her left hand. I unravelled some toilet paper and wet it under the tap in the hand basin.

Kneeling on the linoleum floor in front of her, I started cleaning the protruding thumb with the damp clump of paper. I noticed her breasts and nipples under the threadbare cotton of the nightie, and I saw that her lean thighs were smeared with blood. Her face, curtained by her hair, was streaked with tears.

Mum was closer to my age than to Dad's. She once told me that she had cried on her wedding day at the registry office in Tallinn. She had already been pregnant with me. Even though Dad was raised in the country,

Mum said, she had been the naïve one.

When I finished cleaning the blood from her thumb, I could see teeth marks in the flesh. I found some gauze and a bandage in the vanity cupboard. Mum let go of the wounded part, and I wrapped up the thumb and then her whole hand. While I was still on my knees putting on the bandage clip she said, 'Thank you,' without looking at me. I could smell the cask wine on her breath. She wiped her nose on the back of her undamaged hand.

I sat next to her on the edge of the bath and put my arm around her shoulders. She stopped crying and leaned into me, cradling her bandaged hand in her lap and looking at it there. I had my boxer shorts on—it was a hot night—and I could see our legs next to each other: mine covered with hair, hers hairless. The dried blood from her thumb was still on her thighs, and I noticed a line of snot drying on the forefinger of her right hand. I thought about wetting some more toilet paper and wiping it over her legs.

My hand on the skin of Mum's upper arm began to feel clammy. I looked up and saw that the old full-length mirror on the wall opposite was reflecting everything we did. Dressed only in my boxers, with my chest bare, I looked startlingly naked.

I helped Mum up and led her back into her bedroom. The light was still on, and Dad was flat on his back and snoring. The blood had dried on the skin around his mouth, and his face was lined and whiskery. I helped Mum into her side of the bed. She smiled up at me from her pillow as I pulled the sheet up to her breasts. She lifted her bandaged hand and placed it on top of the sheet.

'You can go to bed now, my son,' she said, and closed her eyes. Her long dark hair had spread over the pillow. I looked at her for a while longer and then at Dad, whose mouth was sagging open. The maroon curtains above their bed head had come unhitched from the track in places. I flicked the light switch on my way out.

Back in my bed, staring into the darkness near the ceiling and listening to Dad snoring from across the hallway, I started to think about 'The Red Wheelbarrow'. That day I had been to a first-year lecture—the last one for the year—on the poetry of William Carlos Williams. The lecturer, an American called Julian Raphael who had thinning hair and wore black-rimmed glasses, had started the lecture by reading in his careful drawl: 'So much depends upon a red wheelbarrow glazed with rain water beside the white chickens.'

When he was drunk Dad often said, 'Every dog has its day.' In the evenings, he would sit at the kitchen table, swallowing beer straight from one brown longneck after another. Mum drank cask wine out of a tumbler—to keep him company, she said. Sometimes they played canasta as they drank, but usually they just drank. I sat in my bedroom, doing homework or watching my old TV.

Mum and Dad didn't talk much, but after Dad started to get drunk he liked to repeat phrases. 'Every dog has its day' was one of them. He also told Mum, 'You're a slut,' and, 'You're an idiot.' As the evenings went on, he tended to get louder, until sometimes he was screaming and spitting on the crocheted tablecloth. Bottles were smashed down on the old wooden table beneath, or sometimes thrown at the wall or on the floor. Now and then he laid into her.

Earlier in the year, when I started my arts degree, I looked up the phrase 'every dog has its day' in a dictionary of literary quotations in the university library, and found it attributed to an English book that sounded academic and that I doubted Dad had ever read. I had never seen Dad read.

Among the few books that Mum and Dad had in the house were my old Jacaranda world atlas from school

and two fat English dictionaries. Mum kept them on top of the fridge for when she did the crossword in the newspaper in the mornings. She was trying to improve her English, she said, so that one day she might get a job. There was also a set of encyclopaedias that Mum kept stacked behind her shoes in her bedroom cupboard after Dad, one night, had torn some of the pages and covers from their spines. Mum had purchased them from a door-to-door salesman for me when I started high school, and Dad had been angry about it.

I thought that the phrase about dogs was probably about revenge, but I didn't know why Dad wanted revenge. I didn't know on whom he wanted revenge. He never spoke about his life in Estonia. Earlier in the year I had asked him, after a history lecture on socialism, what it was like to live in a communist country. He had said it was like any other life.

Mum told me the stories that her father, a schoolteacher and a widower, had told her about the war: how her grandfather was among the thousands deported to labour camps by the Soviets and never seen again; how the Germans brought in Jews, planning to use the Baltic countries for their extermination plans. Things were already different, Mum said, by the time she was growing up in the 1970s and '80s. When she got her first job, at the Tallinn Central Post Office in 1990, formal independence was only a year off.

That was when she met Dad. She fell pregnant, they got married, and they left for Australia. Her father had died suddenly of a heart attack, and she didn't have anything keeping her there.

On the mantelpiece above the fireplace in our living room was a photograph of Mum and Dad at the registry office on their wedding day. Dad was already forty. His blond hair is parted to the side, and he is looking at Mum with large eyes. Mum is looking at the camera. She is half his age, dark-haired and beautiful.

There was another photograph on the mantelpiece— the only other one we had of Dad in Estonia—which was taken when he was younger. Dad worked as a mail carrier, and in the picture he is wearing the uniform of the Estonian postal service. He has a crew cut, and he is squinting and pointing a pistol at an unseen target in the surrounding forest. There is a large black dog sitting on the grass next to him with its head raised, and a hessian sack on the ground behind them.

Mum said that Dad turned on her when they arrived in Australia. She couldn't account for the change. She

didn't know much about Dad's life before they met, and she knew little about his childhood. She did know that, like her, he was an only child. Both of his parents had been alive, but his father, Mum said, was often away.

She told me that Dad's upbringing was primitive. She used the word as if it was dirty. He had lived in a house in the woods. He had slept on a mattress filled with hay. During winter he had shat with the animals in the barn, where it was warm. It had been his job, she told me, to kill chickens for the table.

I had a nine o'clock tutorial on William Carlos Williams. When I got up at seven-thirty, Mum and Dad were still asleep in the curtained darkness of their bedroom. Mum had turned onto one side. I could see her bandaged fist, curled near her chest. Dad was still on his back, snoring. There was a recession, and he had been laid off from the stamping plant in Altona. Even from the doorway Mum and Dad's bedroom stunk of their bodies and stale alcohol. I closed their door and went into the bathroom.

The morning sun was bright against the frosted glass of the window. I picked up the bloodied paper that I had dropped on the floor the night before and threw it into the toilet bowl. There were bloodstains, so I wet a fresh wad of toilet paper and started to clean the bath's edge and the floor.

When I was on my knees I saw that one smudge of blood had a toe print in it that could only be Mum's. She had small feet. I liked to watch her paint her toenails, which she did Saturday nights after a bath, wearing her white bathrobe and with her hair wound in a towel. She would sit on a kitchen chair, her toes curled over the edge of the wooden table and its crocheted cloth, carefully brushing red polish on each nail.

From the floor of the bathroom I saw myself exposed in the full-length mirror again, still dressed in my boxer shorts. The silver of the mirror was beginning to corrupt in places. I quickly stood and threw the paper in the toilet. Then I washed my face and brushed my teeth at the sink, ignoring the mirror on the wall next to me.

I got to the station in time but the train was running late, so Dr Raphael was already in the room when I arrived for the tutorial. He was sitting at the front of the room, wearing the thick-lensed glasses that made his eyes look small, flicking through his copy of William Carlos Williams' *Selected Poems*. His remaining strands of dark hair were oiled and plastered across his head.

When I entered, he looked up, said my surname in his thick drawl and nodded. He repeated the ritual for every student who entered the room after me, even the girls, which I always thought was a little impolite.

I sat down in the back row by myself. Brendan was, as usual, the last to arrive. When he came in, he was busy tucking his iPod and earphones into the pocket of his denim jacket. Then he sat next to me, punched my arm and pulled a pen from the other pocket of his jacket.

Dr Raphael tapped his watch and announced that he was starting the class. He told us to organise ourselves into groups of four, and then he began to hand out double-sided photocopies. On one side of the sheet was 'The Red Wheelbarrow'. Two blond-haired girls in the row in front of me and Brendan clumsily shuffled their handbags aside with their feet, and turned their chairs to face our table. They looked like they were wearing their mums' make-up. One of them had braces, which made her look even more like a girl.

'Are you kidding?' Brendan asked, as Dr Raphael placed four copies of the poem on our desk. 'You want us to analyse this? What's there to say?' Brendan generally gave his tutors a hard time, and generally they seemed to like him for it. It was impossible to tell, though, with Julian Raphael.

Dr Raphael paused, and then, looking at Brendan with his small eyes, he said, 'I am assuming, Morrissey, that you have done your reading.' He adjusted his black frames. 'You will know, then,' he drawled, 'that there are those who have found plenty to say.'

When Dr Raphael moved on, Brendan grabbed a photocopy and mumbled, 'Some fuckin' chickens and a wheelbarrow left out in the rain.' He leaned back in his chair and looked down at the poem on his lap. The two girls giggled.

When I was sixteen we kept a couple of white chickens in a coop in the backyard. Dad had been given the chickens and the coop by an Italian neighbour, an old man who said he was going back to Sardinia to die. We didn't have much to do with our neighbours. The Italian made his offer to Dad over the high grey paling fence one Saturday afternoon.

Once they were installed in our backyard the chickens were never let out, and their coop was never cleaned. The floor of the coop, during winter, was mud.

I remember, in the evenings, watching Mum, who was frightened of the chickens, throwing in the vegetable peelings that Dad had told her to feed them.

She always looked out of place in our unkempt backyard. She wore heels and dresses that she sewed herself at home. My favourite was a beige one styled like a safari shirt, with a matching belt. She wore it sometimes on Thursdays, when she did the grocery shopping.

The coop was only metres from my bedroom window. I didn't like the chickens either. It was the noise more than anything: the constant murmuring, the ugly cries. I had to wear headphones or put on the TV even when I was supposed to be doing homework.

One Sunday, about a year after we got the chickens, Dad decided he would show me how to kill one. With his left hand and foot, he held one squawking and flapping chicken on the old stump he used for chopping wood, and with his right hand he brought down the axe. The chicken's head dropped onto the sawdust on the ground, and blood spewed from the neck. Dad let go of the bird, which stumbled, thrashing its wings, and then fell dead.

He strung it up by its gnarled feet in the shed and started ripping out fistfuls of bloodied feathers, which he let drop onto the gravel below. His teeth were bared. Dad rarely spoke much, and he didn't say anything then. I looked at the other chicken, now quiet, in the coop. Dad didn't notice when I went inside.

That evening, from my bedroom, I heard yelling in the kitchen. Mum had cooked the carcass in the oven, but she hadn't known to remove its guts. When I went into the kitchen, I saw Dad grab the chicken from the oven tray on the kitchen bench and hurl it through the swing lid of the plastic bin.

'Idiot,' he cried. He grabbed Mum by the throat as she stood at the sink. He shook her for a few seconds, in silence, then stormed out into the backyard.

I held Mum. I was taller than her by the time I was sixteen. I rubbed her slender back, my palms following the curve of her spine beneath her soft dress. She sobbed on my shoulder. I was trying to grow a beard, and I could feel her long hair getting caught on my cheek. Outside, I heard the surviving chicken begin to shriek.

The girls had each taken a photocopy of the poem, which they held on their laps. They were looking at the text, but I could tell they weren't even trying. Brendan, with

his copy now on the desk, was drumming his fingers on his thighs and nodding as if he was privately listening to music. The groups of students near us were whispering and taking notes.

I usually didn't say anything, but I leaned forward to take the remaining photocopy from the table and said, 'There's got to be more to it.'

Brendan and the girls looked at me.

I shrunk back into my chair. 'I mean'—my voice was already small—'what about the red wheelbarrow? The poem says that everything depends on it.'

The girls looked down at their laps. The one with the braces began biting her bottom lip.

'It's all got to mean something,' I said quietly, but I'd already given up.

Brendan suddenly slapped me on the shoulder. 'Man, let's just say that Williams should have stuck to his day job.' William Carlos Williams, Dr Raphael had told us in the lecture, was a paediatrician. The girls laughed—loudly and unnaturally, I felt. I didn't think much of the girls in any of my classes. Brendan, though, liked blondes.

Because he liked blondes, Brendan had come up with the idea of spending three weeks backpacking in Scandinavia during the midyear break just gone. I hadn't wanted to go, but Mum had encouraged me. Dad took all my Austudy payments for board, but for years I had been working for cash on weekends in the bindery of a local printery. I should use those savings, Mum said, and enjoy myself. I could go to Estonia. I could see my homeland.

'Your real homeland,' she said, when I pointed out that I had been born in Footscray. After all, she joked, I had been made in Tallinn. I had to force a smile every time she said that. 'You could see,' Mum continued, 'where Dad and I grew up.' She wished she could go too.

I didn't say anything to Brendan about Estonia before we left, but when we were in Helsinki I talked him into taking the ferry across the Gulf of Finland to Tallinn. It helped that we had already taken the Silja Line from Copenhagen to Stockholm, and from Stockholm to Helsinki, and that he had got lucky in nightclubs on each leg of the trip. It also helped that some British students we met at a bar in Helsinki told us about the cheap beer in Estonia.

The Silja Line to Tallinn was full of middle-aged and dour Finns who flocked to the duty-free shops as

soon as they boarded, armed with foldable trolleys on which they piled boxes of vodka and beer. Brendan was in a sulk for the entire morning. We sat in silence in a passageway lined with poker machines.

When we got to Tallinn there was a grey mist of rain. We were only staying two nights, so we boarded a tourist bus that was taking a circuitous route through Tallinn to the Old Town. The tour guide, who had split our fares with the bus driver, said he would take us to a popular backpackers' in the Old Town at the end of the tour. All the stag parties from the UK, the tour guide told us in his halting English, went there.

On the bus, which was full of Finns from the ferry, the guide spoke in Finnish through a small megaphone. Mum had told me that Finnish was similar to Estonian, but given I understood only a few phrases that Mum and Dad used around the house—put the fire on; dinner's ready—plus all the swear words, I couldn't understand anything the guide said.

I had spoken Estonian as a young child, but I had switched to English once I started school. Mum had wanted me to remember the mother tongue, as she called it, but Dad seemed to like it that I couldn't understand his language anymore. At the dinner table he would always mumble something to Mum in Estonian, and I knew that it was to exclude me.

As the bus toured Tallinn I saw dirty concrete tenement blocks in worse shape than the high-rises around Melbourne. Outside a market I saw old men and women on footpaths, laying wares on blankets in the dreary haze of rain. There were mangy dogs loitering behind them. I thought of the black-and-white photograph we had on the mantelpiece at home, of Dad pointing a gun into the forest, with the large dog at his side and the hessian sack behind him.

Brendan had decided that Tallinn was a dump, but he changed his mind when we reached the Old Town, which was all got up for tourists. The bus driver left us at a bus stop at the edge of a cobblestone square, the tour guide pointing out the backpackers' he had told us about. We jogged across the square to the hostel through the drizzle.

When we got there the place looked empty, but the receptionist, a young Irish woman with dreadlocks and facial piercings, told us that she could only give us a spot in the basement. Brendan thought it was a good sign. We left our packs in the room, which was like a closet with a bunk bed, and went out for something to eat.

We ended up in a nearby restaurant, a centuries-old stone building crowded with rowdy Brits. Brendan soon got talking to a waitress. It was hard to tell how old she was—the room was lit only by a couple of gothic timber candelabra hanging from the ceiling—but she was definitely older than the type Brendan normally liked.

She stood at our table, wearing a black apron over her clothes and green eye shadow. She was slender, with long brown hair. Her English was far from perfect. Brendan ordered a beer, and I asked for a glass of red wine. I told the waitress that my parents were Estonian and that I had come to see my homeland, but she wasn't interested in me. I ended up leaving Brendan at the restaurant.

When I woke up the next morning in the pitch black of the basement room I knew, even before I had switched on the bedside light, that the top bunk was empty. The room was freezing. I reached for my jeans, which I had slung over the end of the bed, and removed my wallet from the back pocket. I dug out the piece of paper that Mum had given me. I smoothed out the folds and creases, and looked at Mum's slanted and careful handwriting. She had given me three addresses: her home, her work, Dad's home.

I unzipped my sleeping bag, put on my jeans and

parka, and headed upstairs. The reception desk was unattended. Outside the mist had become a downpour, and the place was like a ghost town. I could see an old yellow taxi waiting at the bus stop at the other side of the cobblestone square, where Brendan and I had been dropped off the day before. I bolted through the rain and opened the passenger door. I gave the driver the list of addresses, clumsily negotiating a flat fee, and then climbed in next to him.

The driver, a small brown-coloured man of indeterminate age, drove me through drab and deserted streets in silence. There was only the noise of the windscreen wipers and of the car's tyres on the wet road. As we passed a clock tower, I realised that it was very early—and Sunday, at that. With the midnight sun and the rain, the different times of the day had all blurred.

The driver stopped at a tenement building, its small windows as grey as the sky, and then he took me to what looked like a concrete spaceship in the middle of the city: the Central Post Office where Mum had worked and which, Mum had told me countless times, had been built for the regatta held in Tallinn as part of the Moscow Olympic Games. Since coming to Australia, Mum had not been allowed to work. The winder on the passenger

door in the cab was missing, so I took photographs of the buildings through the rain-streaked window, after using the sleeve of my parka to wipe off the fog.

The journey into the country took hours. The asphalt roads became narrower and rougher, and there were endless flat green fields and forests of dark trees. The sky remained a solid slab of grey. The heater in the taxi didn't work, and I felt wet and cold inside my clothes. I started to feel nauseated, and I had to close my eyes.

When the driver woke me up, we were parked alongside a clearing surrounded by a forest of dark-green fir trees. We were on a dirt road, and I couldn't see any houses or other cars. It was still raining. While the colour of the day had not changed, it must have been close to lunchtime. The engine of the stopped car was ticking. I started to panic.

I looked next to me at the driver, who sat with Mum's piece of paper in his lap. His wizened face was turned to me. He smiled. His teeth were bad. He pointed to Mum's handwriting, tapping a dirty finger on the page at 'Dad's home', and then to the clearing encircled by forest.

I looked out of my window, which was still blurred

by rain and condensation. Mum had told me that Dad spent his childhood summers in the woods. I imagined him in these forests, ravenous as a wolf. Perhaps he had shot game or caught fish in hidden lakes or streams.

I had wondered what Dad's parents thought of his escapades, but Mum didn't know. She had never met them. They had died before she came onto the scene.

Mum had been to their house, though. Dad had brought her there after the wedding in a work truck, so that he could collect some old furniture for their flat in Tallinn. They had taken the timber frame of his mother's bed, grey with age but still strong, and a dining table in similar condition. A barn, Mum said, had already collapsed, and the house had looked as if it was ready to fall down. It seemed there was nothing left of the place now.

The grass of the clearing was wet and lush. The weather and undergrowth made the forest around the clearing look impenetrably dark. I raised my camera and took a photograph.

When I got home from the tutorial on William Carlos Williams, Dad was in the backyard setting bait-less

mousetraps on the grass under the netting cloaking his apple trees. There were four trees. While they had been there for almost as long as I could remember, they weren't yet more than two metres high. Nevertheless, they were stuffed full of foliage and green fruit by the end of every spring. The netting and the traps were for marauding birds.

I drank a glass of water at the kitchen sink, watching Dad from the window. It was the middle of the day, and the sky was perfectly blue. It was hot, but Dad was wearing a woollen jumper. His hair was almost white, and it was unbrushed. Crouching on one knee, he sprung the wire on a wooden trap and gingerly placed it on the lawn under the gnarled and laden branches of an apple tree.

The house was quiet. I found Mum in the bathroom in her white dressing gown, putting on mascara in front of the old mirror. She had just had a shower, and her hair was still wet. She had it combed back and held in place by an Alice band. She smiled at me as I stood at the bathroom door, and then she kept going with the mascara.

'Do you need me to change the bandage?' I asked.

She dipped the brush into the black bottle that she

was holding in the bandaged hand. 'I'm fine now, my son.' She smiled at me again, one of her eyes framed by thickened lashes. I wanted to touch her, but instead I smiled back. She turned away from me and started work on the other eye.

I went to my room and ransacked my pine desk for the essay questions for Dr Raphael's subject. The essay wasn't due until the following week, when the semester was officially finished, but I knew what I wanted to write on.

Although English was her second language, Mum proofread all of my essays before I submitted them. I liked sitting next to her at the kitchen table as she talked me through her corrections, even though a number of them were always wrong. She had a slow way of licking her forefinger before she turned each page, and she underlined corrected words or phrases with a painted fingernail. She would be so close that I could smell her hair and her breath.

I found the question sheet and sat at my desk. 'In poems such as "The Red Wheelbarrow",' I read, 'William Carlos Williams strips the world bare of meaning. Discuss.' I looked out of the window above my desk and into the backyard. The sky was cloudless, and the air

was still. Dad, his face set in a grimace, was down on all fours on the grass beneath the leafy branches of an apple tree, setting another empty trap.

Three Sisters

LET US take a look at this place. Marshlands. All the way to the horizon. The land drained, but nevertheless sinking. Sinking into nothing, nothing but itself. Frogs volleying noise in the grass, unseen. The hazy movement of mosquitoes low to the ground. On a lush blade of green a sleek cricket, blacker than night and—look closely—its antennae twitching. Just think: there must be more of those creatures, thousands, perhaps millions, clinging to the swamp grass as far as your eye can see.

Running through it all is the highway: black tarmac dumped on a man-made ridge. Power poles no longer vertical. Wires sagging. And a tarmac bridge, built without so much as a timber railing. Can you see the

creek underneath? A seam of brown water between banks of mud. The mud pockmarked with crab holes and mangrove-ridden.

There is firmer land somewhere. Land where cattle stamp the soil with cloven hooves. Where horse hair is torn against barbed fences. Where colossal windmills slice the air. But that is not here.

Now, the terror of a road train—listen! Tearing at the asphalt, shaking its steel hinges, like a caged animal, angry only at itself. See how it passes in a tumult of wind. Even the murky water of the creek shudders. Then the swamp grass settles. The frogs resume their hollow sound-making. The cricket has gone.

Look around in the stillness abandoned by the truck's passing. There is a cluster of weatherboard houses. Crouched past the bridge, in the clearing by the muddy creek. See the white one-room bungalow? With the peeling paint and the skeletons of fish hanging from the porch like a witch doctor's bunting? That is a museum.

On the walls inside you will find a collection of colourless photographs. Aerial surveys. A fishing boat in a vein of water, closed in by mangroves. A group of moustachioed men, holding onto the rails of a wooden jetty. Eyeing the camera as if it was an enemy. There is a creature from prehistory, all tendrils and feathery gills, hauled up on a chain next to them. And look: another picture. On the muddy bank, a sorry group of men, almost naked, forlorn as the forgotten.

So much for the museum. Do you see, on the other side of the highway, the white clapboard building? It is the roadhouse. The only one for miles around. There is the concrete driveway with oil stains, and the fuel pump, shaped like a teapot, in front. And out to the side, almost lost to the mangroves crawling up from the creek bed, the remnants of a playground. A swing, its tyre seat hanging low to the ground, where the mangroves, worming unseen, have pushed their stems through the mud.

Do you see the derelict cottage out back? Three sisters live there. Two of them run the roadhouse. Svetlana, the middle sister, waits tables and does the cooking. Oksana, the youngest, works the register and helps with the dishes. The sisters are pale-haired and towering. They wear white blouses, and black pants usually a little too short against their ankles. They keep themselves busy. When the place is empty of custom, Svetlana and Oksana clean the fans and filters above the vats of oil in the kitchen. Scrape the ice from the

freezer room walls. Do the book-keeping on one of the diner tables.

Svetlana and Oksana are in the roadhouse now. Cleaning out the cupboards in the kitchen. Spraying for cockroaches. Setting fresh mousetraps. Putting the crockery back. Do you see them in there, under the fluorescent lights, on their knees on the worn linoleum?

And what about the third sister? Tatiana. The eldest. She keeps to the cottage for the most part, though some say they have seen her sitting by the mud and mangroves on the tyre swing in the bruised light of evening, when the crickets begin their chirruping. First one and then suddenly more, you know how it goes, until the air is thick with their din.

A veil, they say, always covers Tatiana's face. Have you heard the rumours? Some say that she is the beautiful one. Her beauty deadly as a siren's. Others that her skin is pocked like the creek mud. That the smell of the creek banks, when the moon sucks the tide away, comes from her mouth. That she summons the clouds of mosquitoes, which swarm up from the marsh when the earth darkens.

It is early afternoon, even though the moon, like a stone, is still visible in the blue sky. The roadhouse looks quiet, but do you see the sign hanging on the inside of the glass door? The place is open for business.

Enter another road train, rattling against its chains, crossing the tarmac bridge. This one slowing into the roadhouse driveway. It stops—do you hear with what relief?—by the diesel pump.

Out steps a man with long, uncombed dark hair. Grossly overweight. He strolls the stained concrete with a cigarette in his hand. Surveys the cages stacked on the trailers. Teeming with ugly feathers. Throaty noise. There is the reek of manure, overcoming the tidal odour of the swamp and the stink of fuel.

The truck driver squashes the cigarette underfoot on the concrete, slaps a mosquito that has landed on his hairy hand, and heads inside. There is the surprising sound of the bell as he pushes open the glass door. Like something remembered from childhood.

And there is Oksana, standing erect and solemn behind the counter with its cash register. You can take a look at her now. Taller than the truck driver. Pale-haired. Her colour too wan and her skin too thick for men to believe she is beautiful.

The truck driver winks at Oksana as he passes by, brushing aside the plastic strips hanging in the doorway to the dining room. The ceiling rafters are swathed with a creeper, its foliage thinning, its trunk muscular. There are long windows, framed by curtains of moth-eaten red velveteen. And against the walls are half a dozen tables, draped with faded red gingham tablecloths.

The truck driver seats himself at a table by one of the windows, facing the swinging door to the kitchen. There is a fish tank on a stand against the wall there. A goldfish floats on its side in the cloudy water. Can you see it? Playing silently for time, then struggling? The truck driver cannot. Svetlana has already appeared through the swinging door. She stands in front of him, pen and notepad ready.

The truck driver looks up at her pale face. Eyelashes next to invisible. She is almost identical to her younger sister, though she might be taller. Do you agree that there is something clumsier about her?

The fat man's face grows a smile. Svetlana returns the gaze, if not the smile. Seconds pass. The sisters are not known for their conversation. Their skills, people say, are still only rudimentary. The truck driver breaks the silence.

'You don't remember me, do you, love?' He pauses.
'Although I'm fatter. Why not say it? Nothing wrong
with talking straight.' He looks at his stomach, covered
by a flannel shirt, and pats the fabric there.

The odour of the truck driver's body is mixing with
the air. The reek of sweat. Old alcohol. Seeping from
his organs, his skin, as if he was pickling himself. Can
you smell it? It is hard to tell if Svetlana does. Standing
there in her black pants and white blouse, frilled around
the collar. Her hair sprayed into a bun.

The truck driver folds his hands over his swollen
belly. Looks up at Svetlana again.

'My dad was always one for straight talking. There
was this time when I was a boy. A helicopter crashed on
the old farm. Squashed down onto the ground and burst
into flames.' The truck driver presses his hands into
the yielding flesh of his stomach and then lifts them.
Spreads his fingers in the air. Returns his hands to his
belly. Looks at them there. 'Afterwards there were these
black bodies, out in the paddock, in the long grass. Not
that the cows cared.'

Svetlana waits with her notepad and biro. There is
a clock ticking. The white one on the wall above the
door into the kitchen. The minute hand shudders

every time the clock registers the passing of a second.

The fat man looks up at Svetlana again, slowly grinning. 'Well, just before the helicopter came down, as we were watching its death spin from the back porch, Mum turned to Dad and said, "Do something!" Dad said'—and here the truck driver puts on a mock-Italian accent and rhythmically waves his right hand—'"Whadda you want me to do? Catch it?"'

The truck driver stops, his hand still in the air, smiling up at the tall, thick-skinned woman in front of him. Svetlana looks at him through her pale eyelashes, her pen and notepad poised at chest level. The fat man lowers his hand, smears his sleeve across his mouth. Wiping away the grin. Then he rests his heavy hands on the red-and-white tablecloth, fingers splayed. Begins to inspect them. The nails—perhaps you noticed earlier?—are long and dirty.

'Look, get me a steak, will you? You know how I like it.'

Svetlana brings the notepad and pen close to her face. She scrawls with her blue biro, then walks briskly to the swinging doors, disappearing into the kitchen.

A dry leaf from the vine that clings to the ceiling rafters drifts down to the truck driver's table. Do you see how the creeper appears to be dying in places? Turning crisp and brown. The fat man flicks the curled leaf from the tablecloth onto the floor.

He looks out the long window framed by red velveteen. The swing is there, planted in the earth, just past the edge of the concrete. And the tangle of mangroves, hiding the brown line of the creek. Most of the water drawn out now by the weight of the moon. Can you see the crabs in the mud? Like the skeletons of dolls, crawling silently from grave to grave. And the hovering mosquitoes? The truck driver cannot. He looks up at the moon in the vast plain of the sky.

Into the dining room drifts the sound and smell of cooking steak. Then the fans above the hotplate in the kitchen are switched on. The fat man calls out.

'I'll be right back, love.'

He manoeuvres himself out of his chair and through the plastic strips into the front room. Oksana is gone from behind the counter there. The bell rings as he opens the door and steps out onto the concrete driveway, suddenly bright. He shields his eyes and heads for the fuel pump and the truck.

The chickens sound dusty. Their throats. Claws. Wings. Feathers in the dark cages. Can you hear them?

The truck driver hears nothing. He swings open the door of the cabin. Tucks his long greasy hair behind one ear and leans down to the polystyrene box he keeps on the floor to retrieve a tepid can of beer.

Look quickly: up there! A pelican flying across the highway. From the direction of the museum. Beating the air with its wings as if its soul was old and heavy. It flaps over the semitrailer, circles over the roadhouse. Floats down to rest, flapping and grabbing with its claws at the frame of the old swing. The bird clutches the rusted steel, fluffs its wings and sinks its gullet into the rancid feathers on its chest. Blinks its eyes, rimmed like targets.

From there, the pelican watches the truck driver. The fat man slams the door of his truck. Opens the can. After a sharp crack the tin makes another noise. Like the truck did—do you remember? A sound of release.

The truck driver makes his way back to the roadhouse. Pushes open the glass door, once again triggering that small bell. Thrusts aside the plastic strips to the dining room and sees, on the checked cloth of his table, a brown steak on a plate with a pile of yellow chips. All framed by the curtains of red velveteen, eaten by moths and silverfish over who knows how many years. How long do they say that the three sisters have been here?

The truck driver sits down on his chair. Svetlana is nowhere to be seen. He takes a drink of his beer and puts the can down. Picks up his knife and fork. Pulls his chair in. Starts sawing off a portion of the T-bone steak, brown juice and oil mixing on his plate.

Do you see that the fish in the glass tank has stopped moving? It floats now, waterlogged. Just below the surface. The truck driver, busy with his food, does not notice.

Enter an old white ute in the driveway of the roadhouse. Watch its slow approach through the windows of the dining room. The truck driver, chewing a piece of steak, watches it too. The ute comes to a stop just outside his window. In a spot near the swing, where the concrete of the roadhouse merges with the mud and the mangroves. And then, further below, the creek bed, crabs clawing their way out of muddy holes. The brown line of water. Soundless clouds of mosquitoes.

Can you see that the pelican, roosting on top of the abandoned swing, has turned its attention to the car? There is the squawk of the door, all stiff around its

edges, and an old man emerges. Thin, with bandy legs. He leans on a cane. Closes the car door, which creaks, then bangs. Pats the dog tied by a rope on the ute's tray. The old Labrador, fur like a doormat, thumps its tail.

The old man walks around to the roadhouse door. There is the tinkle of the bell, again like a reminder of something, and then he is inside. Oksana appears at the front counter—did you see her there just briefly?—but retreats as the old man heads towards the dining room. He pushes through the plastic strips with his cane. Walks past the truck driver and sits down at a table ahead of him. Notice how the old man is too polite to sit with his back to the other fellow? The truck driver, though, keeps busy with his steak.

The old man looks through the window between the tattered drapes to his dog outside. He notices the pelican, like a creature from another world, roosting on top of the derelict swing. Then Svetlana is there, pale and large, like the bird, standing at his other side. The old man looks up at her with watery eyes. Speaks softly.

'Oh, hello there, young lady. Steak and chips, please.'

Do you notice how his head rocks slightly? How he holds onto the walking stick, which he has laid on the gingham tablecloth in front of him, his hands mottled and jittery? Svetlana pays no heed to these signs of age. She scrawls on her notepad with her biro. Holding it close to her nose. Then she bustles off, bun firm on the top of her head. The hems of her black pants hectic around her ankles. She disappears through the swinging door. A leaf from the vine on the ceiling floats to the floor.

Now the truck driver, still chewing and holding his cutlery ready, regards the newcomer at the table ahead of him. The old man is watching his own fingers. Do you see how they look? Bony and unsettled, like crabs, on the wood of the cane. The fat man, swallowing his steak, decides to intervene.

'You're English, then. Still got quite an accent.'

The old man looks up at the bloated face of the truck driver, framed in uncombed hair, and then down again at his fingers on the walking stick. The wood of the cane is old and dull.

'Yes, yes,' he says, 'fair enough. Well, Welsh, actually, but yes, yes.'

Like the truck driver, the old man has yet to notice the fish tank on the nearby wall. The dead fish now belly-up against a corner. Do you see it there? Washed out and swollen. Pressed against the glass. As if something— the wind, a tide—had pushed it into that place.

The truck driver, without putting down his cutlery, wipes his mouth on his flannel sleeve. 'My dad had an accent.'

The old man, quaint in his manners, dutifully looks up from his cane. He has a blanched face and moist eyes. The truck driver, knife and fork in hand, slowly grins at him. The same grin he gave Svetlana.

'One time, when I was a kid, a couple of Jehovah's Witnesses came to the door. Two old birds. You know the type I mean. Dad was yelling at them, and the old birds looked all confused. They asked: "Why don't we go out with our wives?" Then Dad yelled louder'—and here the truck driver mocks an Italian accent again, performing flourishes with the knife in his right hand— '"No, I said, Why don'ta you get on with your lives?"'

The old man looks down at his cane. Scrawny hands curled over the stick. There is the sound and smell of frying steak. The fans in the kitchen go back on. And can you hear the chips spitting in the oil?

The fat man's smile fades. He lowers his knife and studies his plate. There is a little meat left, hard up against the pale curvature of the bone. The truck driver stabs a chip with the fork in his left hand and stuffs it into his mouth.

Suddenly the old man speaks. 'Oh, my wife has been dead for years.'

Now the dog outside the roadhouse starts to bark. The noise grows. Becomes relentless as a machine. The truck driver and the old man look through their windows framed in that old red velveteen. Can you see what has happened? The labrador has finally noticed the pelican. It reverses on the tray to get a better view of the bird over the roof of the ute. The rope tied to its neck stretches, grows taut. Do you see how the dog's belly contracts with every noise? And do you hear how with each bark, austere as a gunshot, there is an echo? The noise ricocheting between the mangroves and the roadhouse wall. And listen: there is another noise. In the clamour, the chickens, hidden within the dark cages on the semitrailer, are beginning to stir.

The pelican stretches its neck, jowl emerging from the oily feathers on its sternum. It looks first to the mangroves. The pocked banks of the creek. The crabs slipping back into their lairs beneath the mud. The brown water from the tide—coming back in now, do you see it?—trickling in after them. Then the bird turns to regard the barking dog.

Inside the roadhouse Svetlana emerges from the

swinging doors with another T-bone and a pile of fat chips. The old man turns away from the window. He makes room on his table. Lays the cane across his lap, still holding onto it. Svetlana places the dish on the checked tablecloth, along with cutlery wrapped in a paper napkin, skin-tight. She starts to move away, but the old man stops her.

'Could you cut the steak for me, please, young lady?'

The old man makes a tutting sound, looking down at the plate. Shaking his head. Svetlana unscrolls the knife and fork in a single movement. Lays the curled napkin on the table. Pulls the plate towards her and, hunched over her work, begins carving the steak. Rigorously skinning the meat from the bone, where there is still blood. Then dicing up the slab of cooked steak. The dog outside keeps barking.

Suddenly there is an alien noise. Inside the dining room. Can you hear it? Wheezing. No. Weeping. It is the old man. Head down to his chest. Look: his shoulders are shaking.

Svetlana abruptly stops cutting. Stands up from the plate. The cutlery still in her hands. A morsel of brown meat falls onto the worn carpet. Svetlana does not see it. Instead she sees, through the window between the ragged curtains, the barking dog on the back of the ute. And the pelican on the top of the swing. Do you see it there too? Its head high. Its gullet bulging. Its wings spread as if for flight. Dripping greasy feathers from their undersides.

Now it is evening. The sky bleeds all the way to the horizon. The frogs, lying in the marshlands, are sending their echoes. The crickets join in. See how the clouds of mosquitoes are beginning to rise as the earth turns to the night? To the never-ending blackness of the universe, where they say that everything—even all of this—began? And look: here come the starlings. One. Three. A dozen or more. Sweeping through the insects. Their noise shrill as panic. Their tiny hearts like ticking bombs.

The highway is black and silent. Beneath the bridge the creek is full, the water still as mud amid the mangroves. The museum is empty and dark. Across the tarmac road, the sign on the glass of the roadhouse door reads CLOSED.

But look! Tatiana is there on the tyre swing. Gently rocking. Her feet on the earth, among the shoots of the mangroves probing their way unseen through the mud.

She wears black pants, like her sisters. But, as legend has it, her veil is on. There is no breeze to lift it. Can you see how impossible it is, in this shiftless place, to glimpse her face, to get a proper look?

Let us leave her. Look to the marshlands that open up just beyond the concrete driveway and the white roadhouse with its cottage out the back. A flock of ibises has appeared there in the swamp grass. Against the evening light. The silhouettes of their black heads like pickaxes.

The Double

SHE OPENS her eyes under a sky crowded with clouds. It looks, she thinks, looks like a child's drawing. She watches the plump clouds drift sluggishly and becomes aware that the lower half of her body is submerged in cold water. The upper half is lying on wet grass. The hair on the back of her head and the fabric on her back are cold as the earth beneath.

She knows that they are the neighbour's white ducks around her, although she does not understand exactly where she is. She suspects that she is too old to be lying on the ground like this, being past middle age, but the birds do not seem to mind. Some are squatting on the grass near her head; others glide on the water near her

immersed legs. Occasionally they flap rowdily or open their orange beaks and let out bleak noise.

When she turns her head in the sodden grass, she sees a silent contraption right next to her, which she recognises as a pump. A hose trails from one side of the pump into the large puddle—almost a small lake—in which her legs are submerged. A hose connected to the other side of the pump crosses the grass on which she is lying and ends beneath an old barbed wire fence. She twists her head on the wet lawn to follow the line of the hose there. There are paddocks beyond the fence that are almost completely flooded. The water is still and dark.

Mustajärvi. The word comes to her. Fear slows her breath, and she feels the cold of the water and the earth as if it is inside her. She cannot recall what the word means, but she sees a forest lake, cavernous and unmoving, funnelling into its black depths the encircling conifers and a steely sky. She remembers an outcrop of granite, an old jetty and the flailing limbs of two pale-skinned boys as they jumped. She recognises them as her older brothers, Kalle and Risto, both so young—though they were eighteen and sixteen by then—and both long gone now. She sees their white bodies shatter the black mirror of the lake. Immediately they are sucked below.

She tilts her head to see the world around her again. There is no forest here. There are neighbouring houses to the left and right, separated by more untidy wire fencing. Behind her are the submerged paddocks and, on a rise in the distance beyond the water, a sprawl of new houses. She makes out the tall and unruly silhouettes of some eucalypts.

The left side of her body feels as if it has been anaesthetised. She rolls onto her right side, leans on her elbow, and curls her legs out of the puddle. She gets to her feet on the damp grass, but when she tries to walk she stumbles and splashes back into the water, like a child. She is even wearing red gumboots. The ducks flee in a chaos of flapping and squawking beneath the wire fence and into the neighbouring yard. The noise hurts her head, and she closes her eyes.

She sees the sky above the black lake teeming with pale birds. The world is filled with the sound of their screeching. The vision reminds her of something terrible. She panics and tries to say something, but then she hears her mother's voice. It is almost a whisper: *Puhuminen on hopeaa, vaikeneminen on kultaa.* She cannot remember what the phrase means, but she recalls

how the words—or perhaps it was her mother's voice—were always a comfort.

She opens her eyes and steadies herself in the puddle. In front of her is a single-storey brick house. She walks clumsily out of the muddy water, her clothes and hair sopping. Her left leg is cumbersome, and her left arm is almost numb at her side. Her face feels lopsided. She makes her way over a soggy lawn to the back porch, pulls open the screen door and staggers through the laundry and into the kitchen.

On the wall beneath the telephone there is a calendar with a picture of a monolithic church mounted on top of a series of massive stone steps. The church is flawlessly white against a pristine blue sky. Beneath the image are rows of numbered but otherwise blank boxes. As she squints at the empty squares it is as if the clouds finally drift out of sight, and the sky becomes clear. She sees that it is an unremarkable weekday in November, a month free of reminders or medical appointments. Her head is tender, and the left side of her body still feels strange: as if she has lost half of herself. Nevertheless, she understands things again.

Her brother's widow sent her the calendar of Finnish landmarks last Christmas. Risto's widow sent something every year, even though Risto died half a lifetime ago. Aged twenty-six he drank himself to death under a stone bridge, the river frozen and the snow blanketing all sound. The police had not been able to find him for weeks, until the weather warmed as spring approached, and the snow and ice began to thaw. Risto's death had everything to do with that of their older brother, even though Kalle had died a decade earlier.

A familiar feeling of dread slowly rises from her stomach. She wonders, not for the first time, what Risto's widow knows. Certainly, on the rare occasions that she has responded to one of the woman's letters, she has never told her anything. She wonders too why Risto's widow—someone she had never met—continues to send her things from her homeland. All she has ever wanted, since she left Finland for Australia when she was eighteen, is to leave the past behind.

The image on the calendar is the Suurkirkko in Helsinki, a church she never visited. Immaculately white, it looks nothing like those churches she had attended. She remembers the old wooden building out in the country where she went for the funerals of her father, then Kalle, and finally her mother, before leaving death behind. She did not return for Risto's funeral.

She remembers the aged pastor who buried each member of her family, and the way his hand trembled when he raised the chalice of wine towards the dark ceiling. He was just a poor man, observing the burial of all those other men and women—so many of them—the voluminous earth having room for everyone. Indeed, by now he had undoubtedly joined them.

She has always found it best not to think about such things. *Puhuminen on hopeaa, vaikeneminen on kultaa.* She hears her mother's soft voice again, but she understands the phrase this time. *Speech is silver, silence is gold.*

Leaving the calendar, she hobbles around the kitchen bench and towards the sink. A cup of coffee, she thinks, might help. There is a cluster of dirty vegetables on the bench near the kettle where her husband deposited them, like the catch of a misguided cat, before leaving for work at the building site. He was always digging things out of the earth—potatoes or turnips from his vegetable garden, often before they were ready—and bringing them inside.

She'd had enough of all that, growing up on the farm. After their exile from Karelia and after the war, her parents—with Kalle then only two years old—had been resettled by the Finnish government on a farm surrounded by resentful neighbours. They had never farmed a day in their life, but they learned to harvest potatoes for the table and sugar beet for the marketplace. There had been pigs, cows and chickens, as well as a horse for the tilling. In winter the creatures had been enclosed in a barn, out of the snow, out of death's litter.

She sees the forest on the edge of the farmland, the branches of the conifers clotted with snow, and the undulating earth of the farm clamped in white. She sees her father sitting in front of the wood stove in the kitchen, drinking. He has just shot one of the pigs for Christmas. How he always struggled with it after his time on the front: the gunshots and their echoes. Her mother is outside in the snow somewhere, taking care of the carcass.

She and her brothers, still children, have been forbidden by their mother to leave the house. They have also been sent upstairs, banished from the kitchen. *Ole hiljaa*, their mother would say—*Be quiet*—whenever their father started talking about the war. They knew by then that their parents had lost their families to Stalin's purges, but still their mother was always trying to protect them. They play cards on the mat in her brother's

bedroom. Soon they hear their father fall heavily to the kitchen floorboards.

Feeling unsteady, she lifts her right hand onto the bench by the sink and leans there for a moment. Words arrive: *Raitis ja reilu ei horju ei heilu.* It was a saying, she remembers, they learned at school. *Sober and decent does not swagger and sway.* She sees walls of darkening pine, and hears a room full of children chanting the words over and over again. She does not understand why that other world, which she left behind so long ago, feels suddenly so close.

She looks out of the window at the puddle in the backyard and begins to piece together what has happened. She had been trying to fix the water pump. After the spring rains they used the contraption to pump water out of the depression in their backyard and into the paddocks beyond. The paddocks were not being used—the housing developments had yet to reach there—and in any case the land was already flooded. The water beyond the wire fence is still and dark.

Mustajärvi, she says into the empty kitchen. Her speech sounds all wrong. The left side of her mouth is numb. But she understands the word—*Black Lake*—and sees the lake from her childhood again, mirroring the forest and the sky. She and her brothers used to go there in the summer holidays, after they had finished their chores on the farm. They would walk for half an hour or so, following a narrow trail through the pine and fir trees, the path lush with grass and mosquitoes. The forest path would end at a low outcrop of granite, and there would be the jetty and the lake beyond, like a black hole in the centre of everything, drawing the world in.

As a child she never dared to swim but she had, now and then, entered the water, clinging to the weathered timber of the jetty. The water was staggeringly cold, its taste like iron, yet on the skin it felt silken. Moss marbled the granite where they would leave their clothes and, afterwards, warm up in the sun. She sees her brothers' white limbs flailing as they leap from the end of the jetty. Then their pale bodies, hovering above the black surface and reflected there for just a moment, are swallowed again.

She looks at her gumboots on the kitchen tiles. Her jeans are soaking. She hobbles into the laundry, leans on the washing machine and pulls off her boots. Next she peels off her socks and pants. Her left arm is still hopeless, but she finally manages to pull her wet shirt

over her head. She looks at the soiled cloth on the back of the garment and remembers the wet patch on her head. She lifts her right hand and feels where her brown hair—she has to dye the grey out of it nowadays—is clotted and soiled. It reminds her of blood.

She thinks of her father, kicked in the head by the workhorse one spring, lying face down on the muddy earth with the blood matted on his head. Their mother had sent them inside. She remembers Black Lake and Kalle. Only she and Risto had been present. That day there had been no turning away.

Standing in her underwear in the laundry, she begins to shiver violently. She rubs her shirt against the muddy back of her head, before stuffing the garment in the machine. Then she limps down the hallway to her bedroom. She finds her fleecy nightgown in a bedside drawer, pulls it on awkwardly, and buries herself beneath the covers. Lying there, slowly beginning to find warmth, she looks at the clock on her bedside table. She has lost over an hour of her day, and there are jobs waiting in the sewing room.

Sewing gives her no pleasure—she learned it as a chore from her mother—but she has always been good enough at it to help her husband with their expenses.

It had been a convenient job when their daughter, now living in another country with her own family, was small. Lying in her bed, she becomes aware of the emptiness of the house around her, but she does not resent her daughter for leaving. She did the same thing—and she does not regret it. Life has been better in Australia. Certainly, nothing has gone wrong.

She feels herself sinking into the pillow. She remembers the sensation of the cold earth on the back of her head, the ducks quietly nearby, and closes her eyes.

She sees her mother sitting in front of the wood stove, knitting under the naked light of the electric bulb. Her mother was always quietly making things: baking bread, salting pork, stewing berries, sewing. Her father is in the kitchen too, his head in his hands at the table. He has been drinking—there is a collection of dark bottles on the table—and he is talking about the war again.

She and her brothers should have been in bed, but instead they are crouching in the hallway, just outside the door, listening. Their mother and father are reflected in the black square of the kitchen window. Their father's speech is slurred, but they can hear what he is saying. He is telling the story again. They know how it goes. Their

father had been dragging corpses out of the trenches, from amid the snow and the blasted earth, when he had turned over the body of a Russian soldier and looked into the face—caked in blood and soil—of a man who looked exactly like himself.

Olen kuollut mies, their father says to the table on which he is leaning. *I am a dead man.* His head is unsteady as he looks up and tries to focus on his wife. *Katso minua*, he says more urgently. *Look at me.* He begins to cry. *Olen kuollut mies.*

Their mother looks up at him and makes a hushing sound. She is smaller than her husband, and her face is leaner. Her brown hair is pulled back into a bun at the back of her head. *Sinä herätät lapset*, she says quietly. *You'll wake the children.*

She and her brothers creep back upstairs to the boys' room. Kalle—he was fourteen then—sits on the end of his bed and mimics their father. *Olen kuollut mies*, he says, his head hanging in his hands. Then, pretending to swoon, Kalle falls from his bed. In her mind's eye Kalle falls not onto the rag rug on the floorboards but into a mirror image of himself reflected in a lake of sheer black.

That night she dreams vividly. It is spring, and her father is shaving outside, his mirror propped on the woodpile at the side of the house. She is watching him from behind a huddle of birch trees shimmering with green foliage and sunlight. Her father has woken late. Her mother has already milked the cows and made a start on the week's baking. Her father, she knows, is hung over. He has been drinking for days, but he has finished with it for now. Soon he will be out in the field with the horse and plough. She sees that her father's hair is greying, and his Adam's apple is big. He holds the razor to his throat, and the mirror glints in the sunshine as if it is signalling. Then her father is gone; only the mirror remains.

Now she is walking in the forest to Mustajärvi with her brothers. The tall, dark-haired Kalle is leading the way. He is about to leave for military service, and he is quieter than usual. Risto, slightly smaller and fairer, only sixteen, is walking just behind. She, younger and smaller still, is following them. She is wearing a yellow smock, which her mother has just sewn from the worn fabric of one of her own dresses.

The forest is shaded, and the tall grass along the path is shrouded with mosquitoes. There are swamps she knows they must avoid, where the earth is covered

with a caul of black water. There are bears and wolves in the thickets and shadows, elk ready to appear in the glades and clearings. *Sinä et mahdollisesti näe niitä mutta ne näkevät sinut*, their father had always said before they set off. *You cannot see them but they can see you.* Not this time, though. Their father was gone.

Then the forest opens up, and there is the lake. Her brothers race to strip off their clothes on the rocks, run down the jetty and jump in. She sees, for a moment, their pallid bodies reflected in the black surface. Then they break through the water and are gone.

Kalle, she tries to yell out in warning, but it is as if her mouth is missing. She can say nothing. The world and everything in it dissolves into silence.

Her husband is waking her, his hand on her shoulder. There is weak sunlight coming through the sheer curtains into the bedroom. It is late afternoon, almost evening. Aulis has returned from work. He is a large man, and the remaining hair on his head is sun-bleached.

Eeva, he says. *Eeva.*

When she looks at him, he says, *Voi helvetti. Bloody hell.* He says it softly, without anger, as if he is confused. He straightens and moves back a little from the bed.

She struggles to sit up from beneath the heavy quilt, her left arm and leg sluggish, and her head sore.

The pump isn't on, he says, still urgently watching her.

On rikki, she says. *It is broken.* She barely recognises her own voice. The left side of her face and her mouth still feel wrong. She pushes off the quilt, positions her legs over the side of the bed and tries to stand up. It takes her two goes. *Raitis ja reilu ei horju ei heilu.* The words come to her again—*sober and decent does not swagger and sway*—though she does not speak them.

Have you been drinking? Aulis asks, even though he has never seen her drink anything other than Eucharist wine—and even that not since her mother's funeral, before they left Finland. After they arrived in Melbourne she never bothered with the church again, a place of gloom and grubby death. They had met a pastor at the migrant camp in Bonegilla. It was through him that Aulis had found work, but Aulis too had little time for religion.

Migraine. She shapes the word carefully. He screws up his face, as if she has confessed something vaguely disgusting. They have been in Australia for forty years, but it is a word that he does not understand. It happens. *Päänsärky*, she says, the left side of her mouth slow and clumsy.

Her husband looks intently at her once again, his face losing its frown, and then he turns and leaves the room. She waits for him to go before she makes her own way down the hallway and into the kitchen, still in her nightgown. She walks slowly, her left leg lazy, her left arm almost numb by her side. Half of her body seems to have given up. It is lucky, she thinks, that she has another half.

Aulis is standing at the kitchen table, where he is unpacking his mud-encrusted lunchbox. His pants and jumper are muddy too. The building site would have been soaked after all the spring rain. At least he took his boots off before coming inside. The floor, though, has a trail of water and mud from her own carelessness. She stops, suddenly afraid, lifting her right hand to her throat. *What have I done?* She almost says it out loud. Then she hears her mother's voice: hushed, almost a whisper. *Puhuminen on hopeaa, vaikeneminen on kultaa. Speech is silver, silence is gold.* She lowers her hand and makes her way to the laundry to fetch the mop.

As she begins filling the bucket in the laundry trough, she thinks about when she met her husband. She was seventeen and had just finished school. Risto, who had been living in Helsinki since Kalle's funeral, had returned home to the farm for the midsummer holiday, bringing Aulis. They had been working together with a construction company. Finland was still busy resurrecting itself a decade after the ravages of the war.

Risto and Aulis, who must have been drinking on the train, were already a little drunk when they arrived. She found them smirking at each other on the front porch like boys. When they came in, Risto nodded to her and then avoided her eyes. He had not been able to look at her since the day at Black Lake. She did not want to look at him either. Every time she did she remembered carrying Kalle's body back through the forest for what seemed like hours, their brother slung like a sack between them—or she remembered something even worse.

Aulis, broad-faced and blond, was different to anyone she had ever met. She remembers how during dinner, a simple affair, Aulis had eaten noisily and then produced a bottle of Koskenkorva with a slow smile. She and her mother, who never touched alcohol, had washed the dishes and retired for the evening, but the two men had stayed up. She remembers how she lay in her room upstairs, listening to the endless chirring of the nightjars and the raucous outbursts of the men

in the kitchen below. Her father had always got drunk alone, and neither Risto nor Kalle had been ones for loud talk. As children, her brothers had even learned to knit at her side with their mother, in the kitchen.

At some stage she had fallen asleep and woken to silence. The midnight sun was glowering on the horizon, and mosquitoes bumped against her bedroom window like tiny ghosts. She got out of bed and crept down the wooden stairs to the kitchen. Risto was nowhere to be seen, but there was her future husband, slumped in a chair. An empty bottle of vodka stood on the table in front of him. His lower lip was protruding, and a line of lingonberry sauce ran down his chin.

When she bent in front of him and gripped his shoulder, he opened his eyes and smiled widely. He reached up and stroked her hair. The sun, even though it could not have been more than four o'clock in the morning, was shining through the kitchen window onto him. His hair was golden. He looked, she thought, like a giant baby.

When her mother died two months later, just after autumn had set in and the world had begun to return to the dark, she saw Aulis again at the funeral and agreed to marry him—if he took her away from there.

The bucket in the laundry trough is full. Relying on the strength of her right arm, she manages to lift it onto the tiles, only spilling a little of the soapy water. Then she begins to clean the laundry floor. When she moves into the kitchen, she mops around Aulis, who is sitting at the table, reading the newspaper and drinking from a can of beer. Her left hand, resting on the mop handle, is mostly along for the ride. Her left leg, while slow, is good enough.

After she puts away the cleaning things she makes herself a cup of instant coffee. She stirs the black liquid in the cup with her right hand, the spoon softly clinking. From the kitchen window she looks out to the yard again and squints. Her head still feels tender, and the slanting light of the late spring afternoon hurts her eyes.

The ducks are floating in the puddle in their backyard again. The surface of the dark water is the colour of skin, reflecting the sky, which is already tinted with the evening. The ducks are perfectly silent. It is as if they are waiting for something. The pump, sitting at the edge of the scene, is silent too.

That night she dreams vividly again. She is on the path that winds between the dark conifers and the pale trunks of birch. She follows her brothers: Kalle tall, Risto smaller. The mosquitoes swarm in living clouds as they brush through the grass. Then there is the granite clearing and the black lake spreading open at the heart of things. How she wishes that she could turn back; how she wishes that she could turn away from it all.

Kalle challenges Risto to a race, giving him a gentle push with his shoulder as he does so. They run to the rocks, Risto falling behind. There they stop to strip off their clothes, then bolt down to the jetty. She hears their feet slapping the old wood. They leap, and she sees their reflections on the lake's black surface before they shatter their pallid images and plunge beneath. Only Risto resurfaces. He treads water and looks around. Kalle is gone.

Then she is under a rowan tree, and suddenly Kalle is there again, muddy-faced, on the bank of the lake. There is the noise of screaming and a vast flock of birds darkens the sky.

She wakes to a silence so complete that, for a moment, she thinks she might be buried. She looks urgently around her. The air above and around her is silted with darkness, but she recognises that she is in her bedroom. The left half of her body still feels numb, but she reaches out her right hand, and touches her husband's arms and chest. He is lying next to her, sleeping soundlessly on his side. On his back he snores like a bear. She puts that summer out of her mind, as she has always done.

It begins to rain. The clamour builds on the iron roof, and she remembers the autumn that her mother died. For days it had rained until the windowpanes were blurred, the farm was mud, and the fir trees at the border of the property looked waterlogged. She had woken up one morning and known that something was wrong. The house was dark. There was only the sound of the rain falling heavily on the roof and on the wet earth outside, but it was not the silence that concerned her. She was accustomed to that. Her mother had become quieter with each death—first her husband's, then her eldest son's. After Risto had left for Helsinki, and her mother had sold most of the farm, it was not unusual for her mother to say next to nothing for days at a time. What had concerned her that morning, after a night of relentless rain, was how cold the house was.

She had descended into an empty kitchen, the wood stove not yet on. When she walked down the hall she

found her mother lying on the floorboards next to her bed. Her hair was a tangle of matted grey and her nightgown was twisted around her thighs. Her mother's legs, she saw for the first time, were traced with large veins. There were new and old sores. Looking at the dead body, she realised that she did not know this woman at all.

All of them—her father, Kalle, her mother—had been strangers to her. She thinks of Risto, lying silent and alone, stiff as a mannequin when the police found him in the melting snow.

She wakes to her husband's hand on her shoulder again. He is shaking her, gently but insistently. *Eeva*, he says. It takes her a while to focus on his face. He waits for her to return his gaze before he stands back from the bed. She sees that he already has on his knee-high black gumboots and weatherproof jacket. Dawn light is filtering through the drawn curtains, and the rain has stopped. She has slept in.

Aulis hesitates, still looking at her, then leaves the room. She gets out of bed a little easier than the day before. She finds her dressing gown and slippers in the closet, and heads down the hallway towards the kitchen, her left leg a little numb but co-operating.

She tries to curl the fingers on her left hand.

In the kitchen she sees that her husband has already had breakfast. The bench is littered with toast crumbs, and the butter and ham have been left out. The newspaper is spread open on the kitchen table, and a cup of black coffee has been left there. The chair is pulled out. He has always been, she thinks, just like a child.

She fills the kettle at the tap, still relying on her right hand, and sees through the window above the sink that Aulis is outside. With the sun rising on the other side of their house, the backyard is in cold shadow. Aulis circles around the puddle there, stops at the raised bed of his vegetable garden to pull out some weeds, and lumbers around the puddle towards the pump.

He is getting old, she thinks, too old for the building industry. Soon it will be just the two of them here, day after day, with nothing between them but a daughter living somewhere else and a homeland they have agreed to forget—if that is what has happened. Their fate could be worse.

The puddle has grown after the night's rain, and the pump is now sitting in the water. The neighbour's white ducks have congregated there again. She counts nine of them, their white shapes mirrored on the mud-coloured

water. They turn on the water silently as if moved about by invisible eddies. Her husband drags the pump out of the puddle, sending ripples through the water and momentarily disturbing the reflections of the ducks. The birds let out some noise but are otherwise unperturbed. They could almost be mechanical.

She begins to make her husband's lunch, holding down some bread with the weight of her left hand and using her right to butter it. Soon she hears the pump's engine start rattling. She looks out of the window again. At the far edge of the puddle she can see the pump vibrating. The day is beginning to firm. The sun, rising on the other side of the house, has lit up part of their backyard and the paddocks beyond. The expanse of water there is glowing.

She switches on the kettle and watches as Aulis heads back towards the house. Suddenly he lurches sideways into the puddle, making an ugly noise and flapping his arms. His boots splash clumsily in the water. The ducks panic, some scattering into the neighbour's yard, others scuttling into the deeper water in the back paddocks.

At the same time the kettle begins to boil, and she is overcome by a sharp pain in her skull, as if her head has been plunged into snow. Closing her eyes, she sees a flock of migrating cranes shrieking across the sky with a sound that reminds her of a steelworks. The birds had flown over the black lake in their hundreds on the day that Kalle died.

Kalle, she blurts into the empty kitchen. She opens her eyes, surprised by her voice, which sounds foreign and slow. She hears the back door slam shut and turns from the window to see her husband tramp into the kitchen with his wet boots still on. Aulis picks up his unfinished cup of coffee from the table.

Kirotut ankat, he says. *Bloody ducks.* Then he tells her what to do if the pump breaks down again. It is perfectly simple to fix.

She puts the sandwiches she has just made into his lunchbox and begins preparing his thermos. When she tries to screw the lid on with her right hand, steadying the thermos with her left, the container tips onto its side. Hot coffee slides over the bench. She pulls back, cradling her useless hand.

Feeling breathless and desperate, she looks at Aulis. He is squinting slightly at her. She wonders, not for the first time, what her husband knows. He worked with Risto for years in Helsinki. They met straight after Kalle's funeral.

Kertoiko Risto ikinä sinulle Mustajärvestä? she asks, her words slurred. *Did Risto ever tell you about Mustajärvi?*

Aulis holds her gaze. His hair is almost white, and there are deep lines in the tanned skin of his face. He reaches over the kitchen bench and picks up the lunchbox, shaking it to shed the coffee that has collected around its base and sides. He leaves the thermos lying in the pool of dark water on the bench.

Ei, he says quietly. *No.* He turns and leaves.

She is at Mustajärvi. She is standing on the outcrop of granite, next to her brothers' hastily discarded clothes. The sun is warm on her head and bare arms. Risto and Kalle are leaping into the lake. She sees their white reflections on the black water, and then their bodies disappear, sucked below. For a few moments she is there alone, looking out at the lake's image of the encircling forest and the hard sky. The lake is vast. There is not a sound. She might not even be there.

Then Risto resurfaces in the water beyond the end of the jetty, inhaling and exhaling heavily from the cold. He looks, she thinks, so pale and small, the dark lake and its reflected world stretching out around him. Time passes, but there is only Risto, treading water, breathing laboriously, and the expanse of the black lake.

Risto begins to look around. His head turns with increasing urgency. She walks, then jogs, down to the jetty, a low structure that juts out from the shore by three metres, no more. Risto, the silken water rippling around him, looks up at her. There is panic on his face. He takes a loud breath and dives beneath the water. He resurfaces, breathing noisily. Then he dives below again, his legs kicking at the surface before he disappears. He comes up again, breathing frantically and searching the water's surface.

She is pacing the weathered boards of the jetty, peering into the water for Kalle's body, his whiteness. Her heart is beating violently. Against the reflection of the tall firs and the glassy sky, she sees only herself—her pale face, her yellow dress—the water becoming murky with stirred-up sediment.

Risto resurfaces with an awful cry. He is holding onto Kalle's arm. He begins tugging it through the water towards the jetty. She can see the back of Kalle's head and shoulders floating, like pale and bloated fish, just beneath the surface.

She falls to her knees on the jetty and grabs the

arm that Risto is holding out to her. It is strangely soft and slippery, and she is surprised by the weight of her brother's body. It is as if something is dragging him down below. She lies down and grasps Kalle's wrist with two hands.

Risto manoeuvres himself in the dark water around his brother, and finds Kalle's other arm. He begins to swim alongside the jetty, a sidestroke, pulling Kalle towards the shore. She gets to her feet and, crouching on the boards, hauls Kalle's body through the water with Risto.

When they get to the steep incline to the shore, they pull their brother's body up onto the grassy bank, leaving a trail of flattened and slimy weeds. Risto turns Kalle over in the dry grass and twigs beneath the branches of a rowan tree. Kalle's face is swollen, the skin smudged with silt, and his body is littered with grass and sticks. His eyes, she sees, are open. Suddenly brown water spills from his mouth, and he starts coughing.

She reverses into a branch of the rowan tree, its twigs pushing hard against the back of her head. Risto stays on his knees at his brother's side, his hands on his hips, gasping for breath, his ribcage rising and falling. He is covered in goose bumps.

Kalle, turning his head from her to Risto and then to her again, looks at them with something like horror. It is as if they have done something wrong. She is just beginning to realise that the black water has turned him into someone they don't know when he sits up and lunges towards the lake.

Risto, reacting quickly, grabs his brother's leg. Kalle falls, his chin and chest hitting the soft earth, but he tries to scramble away. Risto, on his stomach now, does not let go. Kalle's fingers are clawing the flattened grass to the mud beneath. His fingers are only inches from the black water sucking around the long weeds on the shore.

At first she does not understand what is happening. Then she finally realises. Kalle wants to go back in.

She pushes herself further back into the branches of the rowan tree, its twigs pressing painfully into her head and shoulders. Risto is gripping Kalle's ankle with both hands, his face white and full of fear. But Kalle is so much bigger. The thought crosses her mind: perhaps there is nothing they can do.

There is a rock on the ground in front of her. She crouches down and picks it up, and then she moves and brings it down on the back of Kalle's head. Cranes—

hundreds of them, perhaps even a thousand—begin passing overhead, making their way over the dark forest and across the vast mirror of the lake. The noise, so sudden, overcomes everything. It sounds as if the birds are screaming.

Kalle slipped on the granite when he came back onto the shore after a swim. That was what Risto told their mother in the kitchen. She remembers emerging from the forest with Risto, Kalle's heavy body slumped between them, her legs shaking, and her arms and shoulders aching from the weight of him. Smoke was rising from the chimney of the two-storey wooden house bunkered among the tall grass and birch trees. That night, as she lay in bed, the summer sun burned outside her window as if it was the end of the world.

Standing before the mess on her kitchen table, she feels immensely tired. She would like nothing more than to return to bed. Aulis has driven off in his ute; there would be no shame in crawling back under the quilt.

Instead, she starts to tidy things. She moves briskly, relying on her right hand. She mops the coffee spilled on the bench with the dishcloth, then picks up the prone thermos and lid, piling them into the sink with the other dishes. As she works she finds her mother's words sounding rhythmically in her head: *Puhuminen on hopeaa, vaikeneminen on kultaa.*

She realises that there is too much silence. The morning sky has become overcast, and the puddle of water in their backyard is dark and still. The white ducks are drifting there again, mounted on top of their reflections, as if nothing has happened. The clouds are reflected there too. The pump, she notices, has stopped working. She feels suddenly tense, her mouth dry and her throat tight, but she knows what she has to do.

She shuffles into the laundry. Her red gumboots are still lying on the floor, next to the mop bucket. She will, she thinks, have to drain the bucket and put it away when she gets back. There is the mop to take care of, as well. She leans on the washing machine, kicks off her slippers and, relying on her right hand, pulls on the boots. Then she lets her nightgown and dressing gown drop down over them. She pushes open the screen door and lets it slam closed behind her.

The air outside is surprisingly warm, and she recalls that it is spring. In Finland the melting snow would have turned everything to mud, and in places the air

would be thick with the odour of things dead and buried for the long months of winter. She remembers that the police dogs had found Risto's corpse. She pushes the thought from her mind.

She follows her husband's trail of flattened, soggy grass around the puddle. The ducks, drifting on the water, begin opening their orange beaks and softly squawking. It is as if they are greeting her. She would, if she was up to it, scare off the birds as Aulis had.

She stops as she reaches the pump at the puddle's edge and glimpses her reflection in the dark water: her unbrushed hair, her white sleepwear. Then she is leaning over the water, almost as if she has a nosebleed, and she sees that it is a stranger there in the mirrored surface, her pale face muddied, her body bound in white sheeting. The ducks flap gently and make way for her.

The Obscene Bird of Night

THE MAN walked along the street. The winter air was still and cold, and the night was coming. Soon it would take hold of everything, although the city had yet to turn its face completely away from the sun. Already in the skyscrapers and on the streets the lights were being switched on. They stuttered into life against the darkening sky and shone there like talismans.

'It doesn't matter what you do,' the night said in a soft voice. 'I'm so much bigger than all of you.'

The man heard the words but kept silently on.

He stopped, along with a dozen others, at a pedestrian crossing. Mist was emerging from his nostrils and from the exhaust pipes of passing cars. The pedestrian lights switched from red to green, and a belligerent noise started up.

'Hurry,' it said. 'Hurry.'

Stooped in his khaki jacket, holding a gym bag, the man walked slowly on. Snow began to fall from storm clouds kilometres above the darkening city.

'Where am I?' the snow said as it fell.

It drifted onto the road, dashed through by vehicles and their headlights. It collected with cigarette butts and hamburger wrappers in the gutters. Some of it alighted on the top of traffic poles and street lamps, soon hardening on the steel there. The snow settled on the man's head. It seeped through his hair and slowly melted. The man felt the drops of water crawling on his scalp.

'You can't ignore me,' the night said to the man as he walked. 'I'm all there really is.'

The man stopped on the icy pavement, next to a bin, standing aside from the other pedestrians, and scratched his head. He dropped his bag and scratched with two hands, as if he was having some kind of a seizure, until the skin beneath the hair felt raw and hot, blood prickling at the follicles. Then he pulled up the collar of his jacket and picked up his bag. Bowing his head to the growing chaos of the city lights and the falling snow, the man moved on.

He stopped, with the other men and women hunched in their coats, at the next intersection. A delivery van sped through an orange light, hurtling through the slush forming in the middle of the road. There were black letters on its side: THE PREMIUM BUTCHER. Cars cried out in alarm, skidding to a stop in the crushed snow. The van disappeared down the street, its tail lights blurring. The pedestrian lights flashed green, and again came that raucous instruction to panic.

The man took his time and crossed the road. He no longer had it in him to care, but he followed the others just the same.

It was the close of a working day, and the man was on his way home. He had worked at the end of a folding machine for ten hours in a factory filled with noise. The machine, bigger than him, had churned out flyers in a continuous procession. He had packed them into stiff boxes in bundles of fifty, each bundle circled with an elastic band. PRICES SLASHED! yelled the flyers, over and over, as they streamed out.

Finally the machine had stopped, and the man had emerged onto the street, heading back to a wife and two children. Choice had nothing to do with it. These things had happened to him, as they had to his father before him. What else was there to do?

'I know,' said a set of dark glass doors with brass handles.

The man stopped on the street outside the doors, then turned and pushed through them. Inside was a den, warm and full of rank smells. The light was dim, and the burgundy carpet was sticky with old alcohol and urine. The place was empty of patrons. The man felt neither surprise nor disappointment at his solitude.

He approached the bar and, with cold and stiff fingers, extracted a wallet from the back pocket of his work pants. There was a barmaid, with oiled curls and moist brown eyes, who served up a scotch on the rocks and then busied herself drying glasses at the other end of the bar, keeping her back to him. She was older than she was letting on, and he could have made a point about it. Instead, he agreed to have nothing to do with her.

The man sat down on a stool at the bar, letting his bag come to rest on the carpet next to him.

'Thank you,' said the gym bag, which had spent the

day on the concrete floor of the factory beneath the racket of the folding machine.

The bag was holding an empty thermos, a brown banana and half a ham sandwich. There were also two scrunched balls of plastic wrap, a pair of earmuffs and some sheepskin gloves. The man's keys were in a side pocket.

The man looked at the narrow towel and the tin ashtray on the bar in front of him, then picked up the tumbler of scotch left by the barmaid. In the mirror on the wall behind the bar he had a full view of the upper half of his body, covered in thick khaki, the fabric hard as a doormat. He stared.

'What's it going to be, then?' the mirror asked.

The man swallowed the scotch in three gulps and put down the glass. He looked into the mirror and winced. His teeth, vaguely yellow, were visible. It looked like he was smiling.

As he emerged through the glass doors and onto the street again, the man saw that the night had taken over. The city lights were desperate.

'I wouldn't blame you for feeling reckless,' said the night from one of its hiding places, peering from a drain embedded in the gutter. The snow was collecting in dirty, hard mounds there.

The man looked around him. The streets were emptying. There was nowhere else to go. He lowered his head against the falling snow and headed home.

First there was the train station, lit up like a prison camp. The carriage was waiting for him at the platform. When he stepped in, the seats were lined with people, young and old. They all looked sick under the fluorescent lights.

'Hang on,' said a vinyl strap hanging from the ceiling.

The man lifted a hand to it and readied himself for what was to come. The train rocked and accelerated into a high-pitched din. Outside, the world became black. It was as if they were all hurtling, frozen in the electric light, through the depths of space.

Then there were the lights of the man's station, and the doors of the carriage jerked open.

'Out you get,' the doors said.

The man disembarked, and the doors closed behind him, the train carrying the other passengers off down the line. There was carriage after carriage of them. He watched them being borne away, each compartment lit up like a peep show.

Outside the station the man saw that it had stopped snowing. He walked slowly home, past the corner store and the lines of terrace houses, all shuttered up against the darkness and the cold. There were only a few street lights, here and there. Cars were silent along the kerbs. His boots sounded on the snow, which was congealing on the pavement. He breathed mist into the night air. There was no one else around.

The man stopped on the footpath outside his house. He could smell the lamb that his family must have eaten for their evening meal.

'Baa,' the night said. 'Another lamb for the slaughter.'

The man reached into his bag for his keys and let himself in.

The man sat at the table after a meal of cold lamb chops and opened a second bottle of beer. A yellow light shone from the ceiling, and the wooden table in front of him was covered with an orange cloth. There were terracotta tiles on the floor. The man spilled beer into his gullet and swallowed. His oesophagus felt the searing cold, and then, as the liquid spread, his stomach slowly warmed. The beer was acidic and vile.

'That feels better, doesn't it?' the bottle said.

The man swallowed more. It was not enough. He could have swallowed the world.

The man's wife was standing at the sink, slopping a cloth over the fat hardened in the frying pan and then over his greasy plate. Though she was young, she already looked old and tired. Her mother had been like that. He thought briefly of the pretty, well-groomed barmaid, who had turned her back to him as if he didn't exist. Perhaps he shouldn't have let her get away with it, although he knew deep down that she was beside the point.

His wife put the last of the plates in the dish rack, where even his gym bag was drying, emptied and upside down. Then she retrieved a dark bottle from the cupboard and sat down opposite him with a fresh glass. SLEEPY SHERRY, said the label on the bottle. The woman screwed off the plastic lid and poured, her hands still damp from the dishwater. Then she brought the glass delicately to her lips, almost as if it was medicine, and put it down again. Her eyelids were becoming heavy. The man knew that it was not her first glass.

There was a television making a racket in the living room. When he had come inside, the man had seen the children lying on the carpet in front of the TV. The children had eyes and ears only for their cartoon. There was a fire, struggling behind the glass door of a potbelly stove, keeping the room lukewarm.

'Help me,' the fire had called, trying to make itself seen through the sooty glass.

The man had hesitated in the hall. He should have gone in to feed it another log. The cold, after all, was something they all had to contend with.

'Why bother?' said the night, pressing its weight against the kitchen window.

The man saw his reflection against the glossy black. He had taken off his jacket. He looked as wooden as the chair he was sitting on. He grabbed a packet of cigarettes from the table and pushed back his chair, the legs screeching against the terracotta.

The man entered the cold square of his backyard. The night spread out and showed him its things: the rooflines of the townhouses, the television aerials, the chimneys doing their slow work. There was a sickle moon, the clouds around it glowing.

While the air in the backyard was perfectly still,

the clouds up in the sky were moving. They were like something out of a dream. Beyond them was the vast blackness of space. There was not a living creature in sight.

'Don't look away from me now,' the night said calmly.

The man didn't care for its warnings. He lit a cigarette and wandered across the snow-clamped earth of his backyard. He passed the clothes hoist, its wire lines taut and icy, and reached the back fence. He stood there, watching the smoke rise slowly from his nostrils and from the cigarette poised between his right forefinger and thumb. The air was freezing, but the man knew it only distantly. The alcohol had started to do its job.

The man realised that he was standing on his wife's tomato patch. She had taken to growing the plants last spring, tying the vines to a trellis she had attached to the fence behind them. He remembered her kneeling down on the earth, her hair limp and her face shining with sweat. Soon there were green fruit, small and deformed-looking, tucked among the leaves. He had told his wife that he wouldn't be eating them.

He started to kick at the snow with the toe of his boot, until he had exposed the black earth. After kicking some more he thought he could smell the breath of the soil rise up to meet him. It was cold and dank, like the air from a cave.

The man looked at the illuminated window at the back of his house. His wife was still sitting at the kitchen table. The light was yellow and warm, but she sat there so stiffly that she might not have been alive, clasping her glass of sherry on the orange tablecloth.

The man tried to listen for the noise of the TV from the front room, where the children lay. Perhaps the two girls had fallen asleep on the carpet, or they had taken themselves off to bed: that happened sometimes. What did it matter? He too had been a child once.

Just then the night began whistling. The man crushed his cigarette in the snow and looked up at the sky. The clouds had almost disappeared, offering him a better view. There was the moon, sharp as a scythe, and the endless blackness of the universe. The whistling was lewd and tuneless. The night, the man knew then, would have its way.

He began walking across the snow towards the house, watching his wife in the glowing square of the kitchen window. He reached the frozen clothes hoist, and the night fell silent. He stopped.

'How about it?' the pole said, hoary with frost.

The man unzipped his fly and urinated on it.

Mad Love

YOU HAD asked me to marry you in the dark while you were still on top. I had said yes, and you had kissed me on the cheek and rolled off.

Afterwards, lying side by side with you in the dark, I brought up the subject of the honeymoon. The goose-down quilt was stifling, and I could hear the old-fashioned alarm clock that you kept on your bedside table. Looking up at the darkness near the ceiling, I said that we should do something adventurous. Whatever I wanted was fine, you replied. Then you started snoring.

You were like that: content as the pure. In recent months it had crossed my mind that, with your stoop and paunch, you even looked like a monk, although

I generally tried not to dwell on your appearance. Certainly, despite being considerably older than me, you were like an innocent.

You spent your evenings after work on your plush beige-coloured sofa, chuckling at American sitcoms on TV, your socked feet up on a pouf. You ate your dinner from a lap table, always remembering to thank me for the meal when you finished, dabbing with a paper napkin at your lips as I collected your tray. You rarely had more than one beer.

Beneath the stuffy quilt, I felt your semen spread onto my inner thighs. Still wearing my satin slip, I got up and went to the bathroom to clean up. I put my knickers back on and went into your study, which was sparsely furnished, like all the other rooms in your house.

I turned on the down lights. The plaster walls were bare and clean, as were the wall-to-wall carpets, which I had vacuumed that day. In the room there was only a grey laminated desk, a matching filing cabinet, mostly empty, and a set of golf clubs that you used on Sunday mornings. It was cold. I sat down at your desk, opened my laptop and stared at the document icon on the desktop.

I was writing a PhD thesis on the intersections of

feminism and post-colonialism in African literature, still going even after my scholarship had run out, but you had never commented on this. I think it's fair to say that you had never understood what I was doing. You regarded my thesis as one might a genteel hobby, like tapestry or sewing, and you were quietly proud of me, like a Victorian gentleman.

If I had agreed to marry you that night for any particular reason, it was because I had suspected for a while that I would never get the thesis written. I had lost track of my argument; I couldn't seem to put into words what I really wanted to say.

The icon of the unopened Word document glowed blue.

I decided to browse YouTube. Among the recommended links was a news story about a chimpanzee mauling a keeper's face in an American zoo. The video showed a computer-animated re-enactment. The vision lacked detail. I searched for real footage, but it seemed that no visitors—with cameras on, at any rate—had been present at the attack. I closed the laptop and returned to your bed.

In the morning, before going to work at the accountancy firm, you signed a couple of blank cheques and left them on the side table in the half-light of the curtained room. I was pretending to be asleep. You were always genuinely discreet about money.

When I heard your car taking off down the street and the automatic garage door finish scrolling back down, I got up and showered in the ensuite bathroom, pushing the dark hairs that littered the shower base towards the drain with my toe. The hair was yours. You were going bald. Not that it—or anything, really—seemed to bother you.

I knew that you would expect a conventional wedding. You had a large family: both of your parents were still alive, and your four siblings were already married with families. Several times a year, including Christmas, there were dull but cheery gatherings. I was an only child and had little to do with my parents, who were divorced—something about which you had never enquired. You preferred to avoid sensitive topics.

I was wiping down the eggshell-coloured tiles inside your shower with an old red rag when I decided we would elope. I spent the rest of the day in your study looking at images of African wars and famines on the internet, thinking of how little you knew. I kept a box of African novels—the case studies for my thesis—

next to your desk, but you had never taken an interest. It seemed to me that you chose to know nothing of the world.

I made the necessary arrangements with an independent travel company located in situ and went back to looking at pictures of atrocities.

That was how we came to find ourselves exchanging vows on a windy beach on the Atlantic Ocean where gulls were screeching and seals were dragging themselves out of the surf like heavy amputees. It was a seal colony. There were hundreds of the creatures, and their stink was appalling.

I could see three hyenas, or their sloping silhouettes, in the hot distance inland from the beach. The landscape was flat and yellow; there wasn't a tree or a building in sight. It looked like the apocalypse. I knew that, even in your wildest dreams, you couldn't have imagined such a place.

Our celebrant was the operator of the tour company as well as the bus driver. He was a pink-skinned man dressed in beige-hued army fatigues. His assistant, a skinny black youth named Frankie, circled desultorily

around us, using your newly purchased digital camera to take photographs. He couldn't have been more than sixteen. Frankie wore red shorts and had bare feet. I don't know how he stood the burning sand.

I felt stupid in the wretched wind in my red silk mini-dress and stiletto heels, my hair whipping across my face and hot sand spilling into my shoes whenever I moved. I was sure that, at any moment, one of the gulls overhead would defecate on me. Over the noise of the surf and the seals I could hardly hear anything that our celebrant said. I could see, though, in the way you looked at me, that you could hardly believe your luck.

You were wearing the black suit I had chosen for you and stood in your shiny black shoes on the blowing sand. You were smiling calmly, as was your wont. I held on to the knowledge that, in your funereal suit, you must have been boiling.

When our celebrant finished marrying us, the four strangers who made up our tour group, standing back on the sandy road in the shelter of the minibus, gave us a round of applause. The sound of their clapping faded in and out with the gusts of fetid wind.

We turned to face each other properly then. I was taller than you in my heels, even though they had sunk a little into the sand. Your dark hair had been shorn. I had advised you to have it cut before we left, though I had immediately regretted it. The crew cut made your nose look bigger and your jowls heavy. Your eyes were brown, like a cow's. You leaned forward to kiss me. I turned my cheek.

The wind had blown sand into my face, I explained over the racket, picking strands of hair out of my mouth. Your brow creased with gentleness, as if you were my father and I was just a girl. I was certain, though, that I had hurt you. When I had pulled back from your kiss, your face had fallen. Your look of contentment had dropped momentarily.

In the distance behind you, I could see the shapes of the three hyenas. If we could have heard them, they might have been giggling like mad creatures. The skin on the back of my neck prickled.

The ceremony was over. Frankie headed back towards the bus, and suddenly I noticed that our celebrant, Jacobus, was looking hard at me. He was a big man, and patches of sweat circled the armpits of his camouflage shirt. His bald head shone under the sun. He had small pale-blue eyes. I held his gaze. Then you moved in between us, reaching for Jacobus's hand.

'You've done well,' Jacobus said, leaning down to you and pumping your hand in return. 'Very well, my friend.'

You had your back to me, and I couldn't hear what you said in response. I heard only your low chuckle, the same noise you made when you watched American sitcoms from your couch.

The gulls cried out above the crashing surf. Around us the seals, stinking under the sun, kept up their ululating. I looked at the dark stubble on the back of your head and at the slope of your shoulders. There was a nauseating gust of sea air. I teetered, and a fresh spill of sand entered my sandal, burning the arch of my foot. I looked at your back again.

I realised that deep down I had always hated you.

Our honeymoon brought us to the neighbouring nation where, as I had discovered on the internet in your study, landmines were still being unearthed by children fossicking for stones to throw and roots to gnaw. Those adults not lying dead and buried beneath the earth, I had read on a blog, tended to look at white people with loathing.

When we had entered the country, Jacobus had told our small tour group that access to the wildlife in the area was second to none, with most visitors continuing to avoid the place after the end of the war. But the only animals we had seen, on the side of the potholed sand highway we had travelled from the border, were an emaciated impala, road kill, and an old vulture dutifully perched on the bony carcass. The retired American schoolteacher in the seat in front of us took photographs through the grimy window, but Jacobus didn't bother to stop. Our minibus left the scene in a wake of yellow dust.

The drought, Jacobus announced into the dashboard microphone as he sat at the steering wheel, had lasted thirteen years. Jacobus held my gaze in the oversized rear-view mirror, and then he turned and slapped Frankie, who was slumped down and obviously asleep in the seat next to him. When Jacobus's hand hit the top of his head, Frankie cringed and threw up his hands to protect himself. Then he lowered his arms and slowly sat up. Jacobus, satisfied, returned his attention to the road.

I had expected black-and-white relations to be like that, but Jacobus had disguised things well until then. I wished that you had been awake to see it. Instead, you were asleep next to me with your mouth ajar and your jowls wobbling.

You hadn't shaved since our wedding day, and your cheeks were covered in dark stubble like that on your shorn head. Travel, it seemed, made you permanently drowsy. Given the heat and the jerking of the vehicle, I couldn't understand how you slept.

I shifted, unsticking the back of my legs from the vinyl seat. I was wearing denim shorts that should have been longer. I flapped the neckline of my tank top in a futile attempt to cool myself. I knotted my ponytail so that my hair was not resting on my neck.

I looked back at Jacobus, whose face and scalp, reflected in the mirror, were covered in a film of sweat. He was looking towards the sandy road, which stretched out before the windscreen in an endless line. The bus was descending a slight decline, affording a view of the colossal sky and desert all the way to the horizon. I saw the flat-topped silhouette of a single acacia tree. In the distance it looked as small and sculpted as a bonsai.

The retired teacher in front of us stood up and thrust her camera towards the aisle of the minibus, lining up the landscape unfolding through the windscreen. She stood there unsteadily in her sleeveless dress, the flesh on the underside of her arms wobbling. For a moment I saw everything in miniature on her camera display. Jacobus's and Frankie's heads were divided by the strip of sandy road.

Then the American turned and, before I had a chance to do anything, took a photograph of you and me in our bucket seats. 'The newlyweds,' she said warmly, her eyes crinkling. I couldn't even bring myself to smile. The woman hesitated, then turned her back to us and sat down.

You were still fast asleep, your hands crossed serenely on your lap, your face and body jiggling. Sitting across the aisle from you were an elderly couple from Scotland, also sleeping. A German woman with silver hair, who was dressed like a man and who was probably a nun, was seated in front of them. She was doing a crossword in a magazine. I was the youngest passenger by more than thirty years, if I didn't include you.

Jacobus was middle-aged like you. He had told us, after gathering us all at the airport four days ago, that he had a wife and three sons. They lived in a fortified house in a suburb of the stone-coloured sprawling city into which our Boeing had descended.

He had to be honest with us, Jacobus had said,

acknowledging the armed guards who stood at the exit from the arrivals terminal to the car park. The city—and, indeed, the whole of Africa—was not what it used to be, and our safety would be his primary concern.

You knew nothing about the city, even though it had been declared the rape and murder capital of the world in news stories for years. I watched you as Jacobus outlined various instructions: walk quickly from the terminal to the minibus; keep the windows of the vehicle closed at traffic signals; do not wander off at fuel stops; never show your wallet to beggars. You stood listening courteously, with your T-shirt tucked into your elastic-waisted travel pants and your paunch protruding. Jacobus might have been informing you about the weather.

It had been the same at the border crossing, where we were forced to stop at a boom gate marking the dividing line between the nation in which we had been married and the nation in which we would have our honeymoon. The landscape was scorched and empty. Two men in military uniform had approached from a shed made of corrugated iron, guns on their hips. We were instructed to file out of the bus and stand on the sandy road with our belongings at our feet.

While we were unloading everything, with Frankie

heaving out our luggage, the soldiers retreated to their shed. Then we waited, standing alongside the bus, which was caked with yellow dust. The sun was soon burning the top of my head. Ants were crawling over our bags. I slapped them off my legs. You stood there serenely. The ants didn't seem to be bothering you.

Frankie went and leaned on the front of the vehicle as if we didn't exist. He was only on the tour because he had a bride price to meet: five head of cattle for the hand of his fiancée, with whom he already had a one-year-old girl.

Jacobus had told us about Frankie's situation when we first boarded the minibus at the airport. You had quietly chuckled. Frankie had been outside stowing our suitcases, but he would have been able to hear what was being said. 'Quite the ladies' man,' you said to Jacobus and winked. I rolled my eyes at Jacobus—you were such an ingenue—but Jacobus laughed heartily.

At the border crossing Jacobus paced in front of us in his fatigues, his head flushed pink and running with sweat. Then he stopped. 'These people are tourists, men,' he called out in the direction of the shed. 'They're bringing money to your godforsaken country.' His words disappeared into the vastness of the desert.

When the soldiers returned, they crouched down and slowly started going through our things. You and I were standing at the end of the line, so they opened our bags first. One of the men extracted the birth control pill from my toiletries case and held the foil packet up to the sun.

The German nun was standing to my left. Jacobus, lingering behind the officer, wouldn't meet my eyes. I didn't know where to look. The soldier, still crouched on the sand, tilted his face to me and smiled. His face was broad and scarred. Tears began to press behind my eyes. You've got the wrong one, I wanted to say. I'm on your side.

When I turned to you, standing on my right with the other soldier at your feet, you were as placid as if you were at a picnic. You smiled at me and up at the cloudless sky, squinting and lifting your hand to shield your eyes. I stared at the desert horizon in front of me until my eyes felt as dry as the air and the earth.

All the while, my hatred of you grew.

Unlike you, I couldn't sleep on the minibus, which had no air conditioning and stank of diesel fumes. I hadn't brought anything to read, not wanting to think about my thesis. I watched the desert outside my smudged window. Aside from occasional clumps of yellow grass and the unmistakeable shape of an acacia, there was not a living thing in sight.

I imagined that our vehicle might strike a deep pothole in the sand and veer wildly off the road. I alone would survive the ensuing crash. Now that you and I were married, I would get the house. I could give up the PhD. I imagined the bus exploding into flames as I walked away from the scene. Alone in the desert, I would be free.

For a long time, there was nothing for the bus to crash into. Then a cluster of mud huts with roofs of corrugated iron suddenly came into view. The huts were enclosed by a perimeter of sticks, behind which, as our bus passed, I saw a goat and some dusty-looking chickens. There were no people, it seemed. The American retiree in front of me came to life and started taking photographs through her window.

Jacobus flicked on his microphone and announced that we were approaching a town. We would be slowing down, but we would not be stopping. Our final destination was only a couple of hours away. 'We should get there by evening,' he said. Then he made eye contact with me in the mirror. 'If anyone needs to go to the bathroom, it will have to be later.'

I seemed to be the only one who ever needed to go to the toilet. The last time that Jacobus had stopped, just before the border crossing, I had caught him watching me in his side mirror when I emerged from urinating behind the bus. He had only slowly looked away.

Jacobus had woken you with his latest speech. You stretched your arms and rested your hand on my thigh. You rubbed the skin there. I resisted pulling away. You relaxed back into your seat and stared out of my window. You looked almost beatific.

I returned my attention to the desert outside. We passed another cluster of mud houses, then the vehicle slowed as we entered the town.

Because I had the window seat, I saw the children with missing limbs loitering outside the shops before you did. My stomach became heavy. I felt you warm and close next to me. These were the orphans I had read about in your study. These were the children I had wanted you to see.

There was a single row of stores—a supermarket, a garage, a hairdresser—which looked like a series of concrete boxes, their windows and doors covered by bars. The shopfronts offered no shade. Outside the supermarket was a bare-chested boy without arms, who stood like a tree stump on the yellow earth and watched our vehicle pass.

Beside him were two other children with missing legs: a boy and a girl leaning on gnarled sticks for crutches. One side of the boy's shorts hung limp and empty. The girl had a skin-coloured knob protruding from beneath her grubby skirt.

I turned to watch you. You were very fond of your nieces and nephews, and I knew that you wanted children of your own. Not that you had ever mentioned it. I watched you closely, but you didn't seem to register anything.

The Scottish couple across the aisle, who had woken up when you did, put their heads together and whispered to each other as if they had just glimpsed the end of the world. The German nun was sitting attentively. The American woman in front of us was utterly still.

I looked at you. Your brown eyes twitched back and forth, passing over the view outside my window. You could have been driving past the corner shops back home.

I could hardly believe it. I turned away from you and focused sternly on the world outside. The town was gone. There was only the barren landscape. I felt hollow. It was almost as if I wasn't real; it was almost as if I wasn't sitting there next to you.

That night, sleeping at our campsite on the bank of a slow river, I had a nightmare. We were standing in the desert town that we had passed through that day. I had a knobbly stick in my hand, and I started to hit you with it. The sand on the ground was soft and deep, and the sun was blinding. Even as I struck out at you, I couldn't muster enough strength. My co-ordination was faulty. My attack, such as it was, didn't have any effect. You were smiling in the yellow light. You didn't even raise your arms to protect yourself.

I woke in my sleeping bag, feeling nauseated. You were snoring next to me, and there was another sound outside. An animal was rifling through the campsite. There was the noise of the bin being tipped over, and then plastic and paper rustling.

I had read about vervet monkeys raiding campsites at night, but the creature outside sounded more like a dog. I remembered the hyenas we had seen inland from the beach on our wedding day, but we hadn't seen any such animals for days. The last living beast we had seen was the vulture slouched on the impala carcass.

We had reached our honeymoon destination that evening, as Jacobus had promised. It was a secret delta in the middle of the desert, where a river came to a dead end, never finding the sea. Our group would be going out in canoes the next day, leisurely tracing the river's tributaries as the water spread out over the land, forming hidden lagoons and islands. The place was meant to be teeming with wildlife: zebras, hippopotamuses, flamingos.

All we had been able to see of the delta from our campsite, though, was a low and stagnant river, its opposite bank and the world beyond clogged with tall papyrus reeds. Mosquitoes hovered above the dark surface of the water. The area was malarial. Perhaps, after the drought, the delta no longer existed. Perhaps there was only this dying creek and the pathetic scavenger in the campsite.

I listened to the noise of the animal and of your snoring until I couldn't stand it anymore. I unzipped my sleeping bag and sat up in the claustrophobic space of the tent, which was illuminated by the moon outside, shining through the synthetic fabric.

You were sleeping on your back with your mouth open, your face flaccid and your nose bony. You didn't stir. Your blue sleeping bag rose and fell with your guttural breathing. I may as well not even have been there. My nausea grew. Even if there was a wild animal outside, I had to get away from you.

The sound of the tent's zips was violent. I stuck my feet out first, hooking on the thongs that I kept at the door. Then I quickly closed the vertical and horizontal zips, and stood up on the sand.

The moon looked old and scarred. In its wan light the river beyond the campsite glowed a little, as did the papyrus on the far bank. There weren't any animals in view, although the bin had indeed been tipped over, its contents dragged across the ground in the direction of the open desert.

There was the foldout table and the camp stove on which Frankie had prepared our dinner in the evening upon our arrival. I looked at the circle of empty chairs on which we had sat and eaten our overcooked spaghetti from plates perched on our laps. Dinner had tasted only of the insect repellent that I had smeared over my face and body, but still the mosquitoes had hovered around my ears and ankles.

You might have been eating at home, so absorbed were you in the task. You even had a paper napkin on your lap beneath your melamine plate. Behind you the evening sky, orange and pink, had looked as if a bomb exploded.

Standing outside our tent, still in the clothes I had worn the previous day, my nausea got worse, and the deckchairs and the other tents around me began to blur. I bent over and steadied myself with my hands on my knees. Your thongs were there, just outside our tent, on the sand near my own feet. I remembered what had happened after the meal, and I hated you more than I ever had.

With the night falling, you had gone to the toilet with your torch and a golf magazine. The nun and the ex-teacher had already headed off to the amenities blocks, two roofless grass huts situated about a hundred metres or so from the campsite. The elderly Scottish couple had retired to their tent.

Jacobus had taken his usual place at the foldout table after lighting a gas lantern. He sat there turning over a worn deck of cards, a routine he performed at the close

of every day. He turned over one card at a time from the pack in his hands, gradually re-forming the pile on the table. I could never make out the point of the game.

I was in my deckchair, only a couple of metres away from him. The night was growing cold, and I was dressed only in my denim shorts and tank top, but there was no way I was going anywhere. Mosquitoes floated around my ears and hovered in front of my face like a tattered veil. I was determined to make something happen. I was determined to finally get through to you.

Frankie had been crouched next to Jacobus, silently washing the group's dishes in a bucket of soapy water and putting them down to dry on a tea towel laid on the sand. Jacobus had forbidden us all from helping. It was important, Jacobus had said at our first campsite, that Frankie learned how to earn a wage.

When Frankie had finished, he stood up and wiped his hands on his red shorts—the same ones he had been wearing at our wedding. He was careful not to look at me. He never looked at any of us. Then he picked up a card-board box of foodstuffs and, still barefoot, shuffled off to the bus parked in the darkness. Jacobus and I were alone.

'You know,' Jacobus said, without glancing up from his card game. His bald head was glowing next to the lantern; his voice was loud in the night air. 'I know your kind of lady.' He slapped absentmindedly at a mosquito that landed on his hairy forearm. 'You think you're so much better than your husband, but you're not.'

Remembering how I had slunk silently into our tent like a wounded dog, my stomach heaved and I dry retched noisily above your thongs. With my hands on my knees, I lifted my head and peered across the desert towards the amenities blocks. The huts, lit by the pale moon, looked a long way off. I wasn't going to make it. Nevertheless, I started following the rough trail of rubbish, left by the scavenger, through the campsite and towards the grass structures.

About halfway there, I dropped onto all fours, finding the sand surprisingly cool. My throat clogged with spaghetti. I opened my mouth, letting clumps of colourless food fall on the earth. The ground tilted, and I rolled onto my side and then onto my back under the night sky. I felt the undulating sand beneath me and closed my eyes.

I don't know how long it was before I opened them, but the moon was still there, and a dull litter of stars.

I thought of you sleeping in the tent with your mouth open, gently illuminated by the moonlight. I thought of Jacobus, his head radiant next to the gas lamp. I heard the steady whining of the mosquitoes. They would be feasting on my bare arms and legs.

I tried to get up, but the desert seemed to tip again. Then I saw that there was someone standing nearby. Flat on my back, I pushed my tangled and dirty hair away from my face. I recognised the red shorts and skinny legs. It was Frankie.

He approached across the sand and knelt by my side, blocking my view of the moon. I tried to say something, but my mouth felt as if it had been glued with a foul paste.

'Shh,' he said. 'Shh.' He put his finger to my lips, although I noticed that he was not really looking at me.

I suspected that he might be a fantasy, but I could feel his finger on my mouth—warm and soft—and I could smell diesel and perspiration. Then he removed his hand from my face and started to fumble with the button on the waistband of my shorts.

I was shocked at first. I even felt my lips manage to part, such was my surprise. Then I remembered what you had said. Frankie, the ladies' man. I knew, then, that he too wanted to get back at you. It couldn't have worked out more perfectly. Somewhere out in the moonstruck desert a hyena started to laugh hysterically, or perhaps it was me.

Paradise Lost

FROM THE umpiring chair wedged into the earth like a throne, he watched the fiery ball of the sun settle on a quietening horizon. The sky was like liquid, deep and blue. The air was softer and cleaner.

For those lingering minutes, before the sun sank and the darkness came, he felt he could see everything. The haze of the day cleared, and the red earth stretched further than he would have thought possible: flat as a pan, but with low rocks and spinifex here and there.

Sunlight, slanting and mellow, spilled onto him as he sat watching and made his skin glow. There were only the flies to spoil things, crawling on his eyes and lips, bothering his ears, like the sweat trickling in his armpits and groin beneath his khaki shirt and pants.

From the chair's height he watched the world spread itself out before him. He liked to think that no one could approach without his knowing, even during the day, when he had to watch from the shade of the farmhouse's porch and the heat blurred the horizon. He was sure to see the red dust of a vehicle staining the sky. If the intruder was wretched enough to be travelling on foot, his figure would be spotted emerging from the heat craze, ragged and uncertain, like a body that had clawed its way from a grave.

Night was different. Then, he would hide in the bedroom with its boarded window and barricaded door, the blackness in front of his eyes like something solid. He would lie on the blankets on the cot, rifle in his arms, quiet as a beast with its throat cut.

Behind him was the homestead, with its peeling paint and wrap-around porch, radiant in the final rays of sunlight, only the depths beneath the verandah succumbing to the night. There was the removal truck, which he had requisitioned in order to carry the necessary supplies, shining white in spite of the dust, and its own long shadow on the desert behind. Between the house and the chair was the windmill, standing like a gallows from another time, its shadow tall and spindly. And there was the iron trough. Up close it was brittle along the edges, where the rust had set in, but its shadow was sturdy. The horizon enclosing it all was serenely distant and empty.

When he had found the place there had also been a shed, near the windmill. Windowless and with a level roof, it had looked like a box made of patchwork iron. When he had pulled open the door, scraping it over the hot earth, the stink had hit him first, and the urgent din of the flies.

Then the sunlight had sunk into the dark space, and he had seen the red sand crowded with the carcasses of cattle. So many of them. Ribcages and pelvic bones jutted through the rotting skins; the skulls looked like gas masks. The air was so thick he could hardly breathe. Perhaps the beasts had expired in that heat trap. Or they had lain down to die on the parched land, the farmer bulldozing the skeletal remains, hiding them, before abandoning the place.

He had gone straight to the removal truck and found a jerry can of gasoline, splashing it over the carcasses and the corrugated iron of the shed. The fire had blazed under the sun, burning his face as he looked on and rippling the air as if a mirage might appear. Then the smoke had turned black, clogging the sky like a sign that something was wrong, and there he was standing at the centre of it.

He had fled to the truck, the container still packed, and hauled out of the long driveway and down the desert road, the red dust rising into the sky behind him and following. When he had gone far enough, he had turned the bulky vehicle on the narrow road and parked where he could see the white speck of the farmhouse and the black smoke funnelling up into the expanse of the sky. He sat there watching. He checked his side mirrors for a view of the desert behind. All the while he held the rifle across his knee.

His father had taught him how to shoot, lining up the trunks of eucalypts in the bush beyond their backyard. He was so small he could barely hold the gun steady.

'The end is coming,' his father used to say, sitting on the back porch of the old bungalow, night after night under a bare light, an unwatched TV blaring from a deal table. There was an insect trap, electrocuting beetles and moths, and always a bottle in front of him. 'And when it happens a man will have to kill. Do you hear?' his father said glaring, spitting, pounding the table with his bottle, making sure he was listening. 'To protect himself. To protect what is his.'

The cab of the truck was hot as hell even with both windows open: his clothes and hair were soaking. There would have been silence but for his intermittent shifting on the vinyl seat and the disturbance of the flies around his ears. The smoke continued to rise in the distance. Then the night slowly came on, and it was darker than he had ever expected. He closed the windows and pushed the locks down on the doors.

It was like a miracle, before dawn, when he saw the desert emerge, as if from nothing, and then the dome of the sky streaked with blood. The first rays of sun illuminated the white paint of the homestead, miniature in the distance. The fire looked to be dead. His cheeks were rough and dirty, his eyes grainy from sleeplessness, but he had got away with it. No one had come.

When he returned he saw the fire hadn't destroyed everything. It had taken him a week to gouge a hole, wide rather than deep, next to where the shed had been, for the warped sheets of iron and the bones clean of skin but ashen. He had got so hot digging and burying with pick and spade, the flies clinging to the corners of his eyes, busy at his lips and ears. The sun was burning down on him. He had to tie bandages around his blistered hands before pushing and heaving everything in.

By the final day, he was matted with ash and dust. It stuck to his wet clothes and the sweat on his skin, muddying his teeth and his tongue. His whole body ached. His ribs felt almost as if they were broken.

There was a mound over the pit now. The patch of red earth was flat from his boots but spinifex had yet to take root, though it had been some weeks. He looked at it from his chair, the sand smooth and almost shimmering in the evening light. The sky beyond the truck and the farmhouse was a dome of indigo. He could almost believe that he was somewhere new and beautiful.

He had soon worked out how to do things. Each night he set his watch for just before dawn. Its chiming was minuscule in the black pit of the bedroom, but it stirred him from dreams that left a bad taste in his mouth. He would wake blind, the rifle in his arms, the steel of the barrel cold no matter how hot the night was. The wire of the cot's base was hard against his back through the pile of woollen blankets, though he slept with his clothes— and boots—on.

He waited and watched until the crepuscular light filtered through the sight hole and gun port he had drilled in the boarded window, softening the blackness until the perimeters of the bedroom emerged: the ceiling, the shapes of the supply boxes stacked against the walls, the bureau obstructing the bedroom door. He had filled its drawers with sand.

With the night receding he got up, leaned his back against the side of the bureau, and shoved until it slid across the sandy floorboards and cleared the door, the noise always regrettable. He wedged the butt of the rifle into his armpit and lowered the barrel towards the floor, finger on the trigger. He silently opened the door and stepped into the hall. There were two bedrooms to check and then the bathroom, with its sink and toilet bowl stained red. After that, there was the kitchen and the living room.

In room after room the colourless light of the early morning filtered through the planks he had nailed across the windows. The house was mostly empty, but for the bones of furniture left behind: bed frames, a grey wooden table; one chair still upright, one collapsed in front of the stove in the kitchen. He had never bothered to pick it up. All the cupboards were cleaned out, their doors still open. The only sound was his boots on the floorboards.

After securing the interior he removed the barricade of supplies from the west door and entered the dawning world, the desert and sky beyond the porch immense, calm and deep in shadow like the time before a storm. The windmill and umpiring chair were perched stiffly in the distance. There was the squat iron trough.

The air was never any cooler outside than in, the flies already lazily finding him. He would begin his patrol of the porch encircling the house, his boots hard on the weathered boards, heading around the corner to the south and then the east. The horizon there was vivid, and the sky streaked as if there had been missiles.

When it came to the north, where the truck blocked the view from the porch, he stepped off the boards onto the sand, knelt down and slid onto a crackly tarpaulin pegged under the container of the removal truck, training the sights of the gun over the dim earth to the horizon. The ground was hard as rock beneath his elbows and hips.

He would keep up the circuit around the house as the light and heat solidified, the back of his shirt wet and matted in flies, a living stain. From time to time he sat against the flaking boards of the house, the rifle across his knees, the flies swarming to his face and ears. At the north side of the house he got to lie down on the tarpaulin under the truck, though by early morning it was hotter near the ground. Waves of heat rose from the flat earth in his rifle's sights as if the sand was on fire, and the red grit, which had seeped onto the tarpaulin, got in his eyes and between his teeth.

Every now and then he went back inside to empty his bladder or bowels. He checked the bedroom and its boxes. He ate or drank a little, straight out of a tin or bottle. Some days he would shave and wash in a puddle released into the bath from the rusty tap and put on fresh clothes.

Every evening, before sunset, he would carry his rifle out to the umpiring chair. He couldn't sit there during the day. Even with an umbrella taped to the back it got too hot. But dusk, when he could take his place upon the seat, had come to mark his days, the desert and sky softly revealing themselves to him then. The slanting light of the sun made the galvanised steel of the chair shine, and he felt how it buffed his face golden.

He would rest his rifle across the arms of the seat so that it formed a rigid bar that he leaned on. Sitting there reminded him of being on a carnival ride: strapped to a seat swinging pendulously from the hub of a perpendicular wheel, going round and round. It must have been his mother who had taken him to the fair, but he couldn't see her. He had never been able to see her. In his mind's eye the fairground beneath was empty as the desert, as if mothers hadn't been invented yet.

He remembered the night he had finally asked his father about her. His father had moved fast, hurling his bottle through the TV on the deal table. The screen had cascaded glass onto the porch, forming an instant pile of rubble. 'You ungrateful bastard,' his father had raged into the silence and ruin. Then he grew red, as if something inside was swelling, and pitched off his chair onto a scattering of electrocuted moths and beetles. It looked like he was dead.

He shifted in the umpiring chair, lifted an elbow from the rifle, and slapped with a cupped hand at the flies near his ear. He caught one of the creatures between his palm and cheek, but it managed to roll away.

The chair hadn't been part of his plan. He had spotted it from the truck when he was already days into his escape, heading fast down a deserted highway, the sky above massive. He had suddenly come upon a line of craggy houses on his right and, on the other side of the bitumen, a dusty expanse of earth bounded by a fencing rail.

He had already passed the tennis court, thistles fracturing the asphalt, when he glimpsed the shining chair presiding over all the ruin. He had pulled over and reversed, still getting used to the side mirrors and the size of the cumbersome vehicle. Then he had waited for the dust on the roadside to settle, to check that no one was around.

The gate to the tennis court was locked, but there was a gaping hole in the fence where the mesh had curled up from the steel frame at the level of the ground. He crouched and made his way through, brushing away the flies that flocked to his face whenever he emerged from the cab. There were two waist-high posts embedded in the asphalt, across which a net had once been strung, but the chair was freestanding.

It didn't look so good close-up. Still, he had dragged it across the asphalt and through the hole in the fence. He did that easily enough. It was a job getting it onto the truck: hauling it onto the roof and strapping it down. The sun was beating down on him, and the white duco burned his hands every time he clambered up over the cab.

When he had finished, there was a rope encircling the rectangular container of the truck. The chair, on its side, was strapped to the top. It resembled an infant's seat.

In the low sunlight of the evening, he leant over the rifle and let his eyes follow the lustrous steel of the arms of the chair to the red ground. The galvanising was holding up, but the vinyl seat had faded and crisped. He spread his legs, the khaki fabric of his pants catching on a tear. He fingered the jagged edges of the vinyl between his thighs and touched the discoloured foam that had been exposed.

He thought about the last time that he had seen his father: asleep in his bedroom with its pine walls. The old man's arms were tucked alongside his body beneath the covers, just as he had placed them.

He had washed his father first, wringing out the sponge, the lukewarm water dripping into the basin on the floor. He had methodically wiped his father's cool and pallid skin: his face, chest, balls, feet. Then there had been the struggle to get the pyjamas on, his father the whole time staring glassily beyond him.

At first he had thought that it was a trick. A test or trap. He had thought it again standing at the bedroom doorway, after putting away the basin and sponge. His father's eyes were closed, but his mouth was ajar, revealing his dentures.

He had trodden softly across the carpet, inserted his fingers between the slack lips and pulled out the teeth, letting them click into the empty ashtray on the bedside table. Then he had wiped his fingers on his pants, turned off the bedside light and walked out. The removal truck was already packed in the driveway.

Sitting on the chair in the fading sunlight of the evening, he felt his skin lose its glow and become all dull sweat. He batted the flies that had gathered at the corners of his eyes and, as they settled again, watched the ball of the sun finally sink beneath the horizon, leaving behind only a distant slash of red. The sky above it was bruised, and the darkness all around was thickening.

He turned his head, and looked at the truck and the house, his supplies divided between them in case there was a fire or he needed to flee. Their shadows on the sand had gone, merging with the night as it took over the land. There were no stars and no satellites, nothing in the heavens.

A warm breeze sifted through his hair and lifted the sweat from his skin. Not the flies, though. They always managed to stick with him. The windmill creaked once, its wheel shifting in the stirring air. He had heard it once or twice before. He slung the rifle over his shoulder, climbed down onto the sand and started back to the house under a charcoal sky, on the track worn into the lean earth by his walking. The red of the horizon glowered behind him.

He passed the windmill, its stiff wheel looming, then the low mound of earth where the remnants of the shed and its carcasses were buried. He heard the sound of his feet on the hard sand and felt his heart at work in his chest. He had to be quick. There were still things he had to do: check the padlock on the back of the truck, barricade the doors to the house.

Ahead of him the shapes of the homestead and the truck were being absorbed by the encroaching night. Another gust of air, coming from the emptiness of the darkening land, pushed against his chest, stung his eyes with sand and dried his lips. It even stopped the murmuring flies.

The windmill clunked, and then its wheel began to churn. It was more noise than he had ever heard out here. He stopped and turned. Against the red gash of the horizon, he saw the outline of the windmill. And there was the chair. Like a piece of space junk, it had fallen to the earth.

The Interpretation of Dreams

I STARTED to have nightmares about Amelia the night after I met her. The dreams were always the same. I would answer the kitchen phone and Amelia would be on the other end of the line. I knew that it was her, even though she never said anything. The room would become black, and the silence in the receiver would thicken until I felt I was connected to some dark place underground. Then I would begin to feel that the dark space was actually inside me. That's when things started to get confusing, and I would wake up, scared and alone.

If Amelia was quiet in my dreams, in real life she talked a lot. I met her on a Monday morning in a double

period of Year Eleven literature class. Amelia was a new student. Mr Needleman—all the cool kids called him Tony—introduced her to the classroom with his arm around her waist. He always liked to get his arm around some girl, but you could tell he was never serious. The girls seemed to like the extra attention. I had never heard of anything being taken further than that, though girls didn't exactly have a habit of confiding in me—at least, not before Amelia came along.

I had overheard some boys talking about how they had seen Mr Needleman flirting with Year Twelve girls at a party. It was a local football club event, something to which I would never be invited. I had also heard that Mr Needleman was a devout Christian—and he did wear a gold cross on a chain around his neck. Mr Needleman favoured open-collar shirts, and the crucifix was always visible, nestled in the dark bush of hair on his chest. Sometimes, when Mr Needleman was busy writing on the blackboard, the hair there got powdered by chalk dust. At lunchtime he went jogging down the street in his football shorts and an oversized singlet, which exposed his hairy legs and armpits.

Like most of the kids, I thought he was great. I put in extra work on my literature assignments, and I liked to think that, because I was the smartest kid in the class, he and I had a special relationship.

Amelia didn't look like she was going to be much of a rival. She stood at the front of the classroom, her brown hair in pigtails tied with pink ribbons. She had on purple eye shadow and shiny lip gloss. Her silver baby-doll dress was the shortest that I had ever seen. Mr Needleman's arm, firm around her waist, hitched the dress up even further on one side so that her underpants were almost visible.

Amelia's arms were naked, despite it being winter, and she wore skin-coloured fishnet stockings and what could have been her mother's stilettos. The shoes were silver, like her dress, but clearly too big. For our high school, in a country town, the look was completely wrong. The local girls, in their jeans and football scarves, were sure to hate her.

I don't know how the other boys in the class felt, but Amelia confused the hell out of me. She was chubby in the way of a toddler, but she had large breasts. They formed a shelf across her chest beneath the shiny dress.

Mr Needleman assured Amelia that we would all be welcoming, giving her a squeeze, and directed her to sit at the back, next to me. It was the only free spot in class.

I was to share my copy of *King Oedipus* until Amelia had time to purchase her own one.

Without looking at her, I pushed the play across the table until it was roughly between us. The cover had a photograph of an actor in a stage play. He had his eyes closed, and there was blood covering his cheeks.

Every time I looked at the picture I thought of my dad. I think it was because of the time he sat me in his study and explained that Mum had been institutionalised. There were tears in his eyes, but he held it together and didn't actually cry.

Mum had developed problems shortly after I was born—postnatal depression, Dad said, then anorexia—and Dad was the one who had wanted kids. Dad said that we were not to blame. The doctors had told him that, and Dad thought it was important that we remember it. The best we could do was to go on with life as we normally would.

Dad certainly seemed innocent to me, and he set an example by getting on with his routine. He was an optometrist and was kept busy with his practice. After Mum was hospitalised, his receptionist would come over on weeknight evenings and cook us our dinner and wash up, while Dad listened to records and played guitar in his study. Once a fortnight the receptionist came over to clean. Things ended up staying pretty normal, and it was all thanks to Dad.

Each literature class we painstakingly read a section of Sophocles' play. That day Mr Needleman went over what we had learned so far—probably for Amelia's benefit—detailing how King Oedipus had defeated the Sphinx, a nightmarish creature who was half woman and half bird, and who had been terrorising the men of Thebes. Now misfortune again plagued his city, and Oedipus was trying to uncover the source of the problem. Oedipus didn't know, but he had done something monstrous, marrying his own mother. Mr Needleman talked about the importance of irony before we got ready to start reading out loud.

Some of the boys were barely literate, being interested more or less exclusively in football, so Mr Needleman typically asked me to read. I had a good deep voice now, even though it had broken late. I used to yell myself hoarse in my bedroom after school, in the hour until Dad or his receptionist arrived, trying to force my voice to break. I would yell for ten elephants—Dad had taught me to count seconds like that when I was a kid—pause for ten elephants, then yell again. My

throat would get so sore that it would hurt to swallow.

Mr Needleman gave us a page number, and I creased my book open there so that both Amelia and I could see. We were up to the bit where Oedipus has accused Creon of spreading rumours about him. Creon tells Oedipus that he's unlikely to be a traitor, given that he's not interested in being the king, and likes his life of pleasure and irresponsibility.

Because it was a long speech, Mr Needleman said that he would read Creon's role. He asked me to read the supposedly ironic Oedipus bits in which our tragic hero remains ignorant of everything.

I kept my eyes on the play and, to begin with, didn't miss anything. However, Amelia moved her chair right up next to mine, and she leaned over the book so that our heads were almost touching, and the whole time I could hear her breathing. It sounded as if her nose was slightly blocked. One of her brown pigtails and its pink ribbon hung over the pages of the play.

There was the smell of her—something I didn't recognise, although it reminded me of babies. It might have been talcum powder. My mum, whom I had to kiss at the beginning and end of her visits home on weekends, smelled of stale sick or hospital antiseptic. Then I realised that I could see Amelia's fleshy thighs trapped in skin-coloured fishnet stockings under the desk, and it made me think of how I had seen Mum naked.

It was during one of her weekend stays—quite late on a Saturday night—and she had been standing in front of the full-length mirror in her bedroom, looking at her reflection. Dad was in his study practising chords on his guitar, and Mum had probably assumed that I was asleep. I had changed into my pyjamas and was heading to the bathroom when I saw everything.

Her legs were the shapes of their bones. She had no bum. Her ribcage was exposed and her breasts had shrivelled like dried fruit. Her skin was grey, and she looked like something out of the concentration camps that I had learned about in history class—only she had done this to herself. Her pubic hair was blond and fuzzy.

Mum froze when she caught me in the hallway outside her door, our eyes connecting in the reflection. In the long oval of the mirror she struck me as unnaturally tall. It looked like she was watching me with an expression of triumph.

I ran to my bedroom and hid under my *Star Wars* doona, the one with Luke Skywalker holding his

lightsaber above his head, which I had had since primary school. I thought I could hear Mum crying. I squashed the pillow over my head and closed my eyes.

I hated to think about it; I tried not to think about any of it. Nevertheless, looking at Amelia's criss-crossed flesh, I missed the next line of the play.

'Oedipus?' Mr Needleman said. I could feel my face flush red and hot with shame. There were giggles around the class.

I started to read again. *'You speak to me as if I were a fool!'* I kept my voice even, but it was too late. I had given myself away.

After class Amelia followed me to the lockers. Mine was part of a group that lined the wall inside the corridor of the science building, where the air smelled of gas and vinegar. I had my literature books and pencil case in my hands; Amelia had nothing.

She stood behind me as I fumbled with my key. I opened the door of the steel locker and carefully placed the books against the back wall. I rearranged them so that the literature ones were on the bottom of the pile. Chemistry was up next. My vinyl pencil case went on top of the chemistry books.

There were other kids around the lockers, but

Amelia didn't seem interested in them. I could hear her breathing right behind me in her noisy way, and all I could think was that I wanted her to go away. Since the last years of primary school I had given up having friends. It was only ever the unpopular ones who were interested, in any case, and I didn't see why I should bother with them.

'So, what's with the twitching fingers?' she said. 'Are you a spastic or something?'

I froze, my back to her, my hands still on my pencil case, looking at the stuff inside my locker. I felt like I had been caught with my pants down. I had this habit of typing out everything that I thought or said, and everything that someone else said. It's not like I pretended there was a typewriter in front of me. I just typed things wherever my hands lay: by my side or in my lap.

I had picked up the habit after learning touch typing in my first year of high school, and it had become almost automatic. I was hardly even aware of it, and if I thought about it at all I always told myself that I was practising. I had actually become very proficient, and it made perfect sense: I was going to be a writer when I grew up.

In the literature class I had typed out Creon's speech as Mr Needleman read it and Oedipus's responses as I recited those. Amelia had obviously been watching the whole time. I hadn't been called to account for the typing before. To my knowledge nobody had ever noticed.

Looking into my locker, I stayed calm and took out the banana that I had packed in my lunchbox. As I turned around, Amelia stuck out an arm and grabbed the fruit from my hand. Facing Amelia, I saw that I was shorter than her by a good head. My eyes were level with her silver-covered bust line.

It might have been Amelia's stilettos that gave her the edge, but I had always hated being short. My mum was tall—and kind of fleshy like Amelia, before she stopped eating—but I had got my height from my dad, who was also small.

When I started high school I used to try to lengthen my body with a set of self-devised exercises, which I performed religiously every night before going to sleep. I tied my feet to the brass knobs at the end of my bed with two pieces of rope, then I gripped two ropes tied to the bed head. Stretched between the ropes, I held the pose for ten elephants and repeated the whole process ten times. By the end my palms and ankles would be burning from the rope.

'Don't worry,' Amelia said, peeling off the skin and biting into the banana. Her lip gloss left a pink rim around the flesh. 'Your secret's safe with me.'

I had to get away from her. I removed an apple and a novel from my locker with my back firmly to her, headed outside, crossed the basketball court and entered the small courtyard that had been created when the new staff room was built adjacent to the old library.

The courtyard, bordered by the brown brick of the library and the red brick of the staff room, was isolated from the rest of the school, though you could still hear the noise of kids playing on the basketball courts and even on the oval beyond the science building. It got quite hot in the courtyard during the summer, as the only plants were some weeds growing through cracks in the concrete, but it was fine in the colder months. I sat at my usual table, which was one of those weathered wooden types that you find at picnic sites.

I saw that Amelia had followed me, but I was good at ignoring people. I bit into my apple and opened Stephen King's *Carrie*. I had just finished *Salem's Lot*, the story

of a writer who discovers that a vampire has taken over his town. The writer ends up staking his girlfriend when she turns into a lustful grey-skinned monster and tries to feed on him. I was looking forward to getting stuck into this next book.

The King novels were Dad's. I had told him one evening over dinner that I wanted to be a writer, and he had taken me into his study and recommended some paperbacks that he kept on his bookshelf. Dad's study was kitted out with office furniture, but it also had a record player, a giant poster of Pink Floyd's *Dark Side of the Moon* and an acoustic guitar on a stand.

Sometimes, when I got home from school and Dad was still at work, I would sit at Dad's desk and pretend to write with his fountain pen. I guess you could say that I looked up to him—and to Mr Needleman, of course. When Mr Needleman wrote feedback on my assignments, he often commented on how good my writing was, and he used heaps of exclamation marks.

Amelia sat down opposite me at the table. I looked up at her, but I made sure not to meet her eyes. I focused on her mouth instead; I did that sometimes with people. Amelia was still eating my banana. She ate with her mouth open, and I could see the mashed fruit on her tongue and between her teeth. It reminded me of the mushy food that I had found in plastic ice-cream containers stored beneath my parents' bed.

It was just before Mum went into hospital. I had been snooping around in their bedroom one Saturday morning when they were out. I didn't know exactly what I was looking for—I was just hoping to come across something secret and exciting—when I discovered where my mum had been hiding her masticated but uneaten dinners. She used to eat alone in her bedroom in those days, but I suppose Dad and I never thought much about it. Dad usually had the television news on during the meal anyway.

When I lifted the lid of one of those containers, the stench was overwhelming, and I dry retched. I never found a way to tell Dad about it. For all I knew, even though Mum was in hospital now, the nest of rotting food was still under his king-sized bed. I preferred not to think about it.

'If it makes you feel any better, I've got secrets too,' Amelia said.

I knew better than to respond. I closed my novel and threw my half-eaten apple at a nearby bin. I missed, and the flesh spattered against the library wall. Amelia

finished the banana and threw the floppy skin, which landed with a thud in the steel bin.

'My name's not really Amelia, you know,' she said, hugging herself and rubbing her plump arms. The courtyard was sheltered from the cold wind, but the grey sky wasn't letting any sunlight out, and I saw that Amelia had goose bumps. I was wearing school trousers and a grey woollen jumper over my skivvy. I didn't know what she had been thinking when she put on her silver dress that morning.

A couple of boys from Year Eight entered the courtyard and sat at the only other table. They were quiet kids—I had seen them here before—but they looked at Amelia, bent their heads together and started whispering.

I wished again that Amelia would go away, but it was as if she didn't notice anything, for she went on to tell me all about herself. She didn't even lower her voice. She didn't seem to care who knew the most intimate and sordid details of her life.

In the weeks ahead, as she took to meeting me in the courtyard after literature classes, she went on to tell me all kinds of things. That day she started with her home life. I stared at her mouth the whole time she spoke.

Her father had abandoned her mother before Amelia was born. She lived with her mum, who couldn't find a boyfriend but hung out at singles joints some weeknights and every weekend. Her mum wore denim overalls and had spiky hair. She looked like a farmer or a scarecrow. 'She's got it all wrong,' Amelia said, hugging herself.

Amelia, on the other hand, had score after score. She had even blown the school chaplain at her last school. That was why she had changed her name and ended up living in the country. Everyone had found out, the kids had written 'slut' all over her Bible, the principal had expelled her, and she and her mum had to leave town.

By the time she had finished speaking, Amelia's pink gloss had faded, and I could see that her lips were blue from the cold. She unfolded her arms and started to scratch at a lump of bird shit on the table with her fingers. Her nails were bitten to the quick. She flicked the shit away. Then she continued to scratch at the white stain on the wood with what was left of her ruined nails.

While she was distracted, I looked at her face properly. There was some powder from her purple eye shadow on one cheek, and her mascara was thicker on one eye than on the other. The parting of her hair

was uneven, and the skin there was white and dry. She was disgusting.

'That thing you do with your fingers is weird,' she said, still going at the bird shit and not even glancing up at me. I looked at my hands on the table. I had typed everything she said.

The bell rang for the end of recess. I collected my novel and stood up, walking out of the courtyard without looking back. I got across the asphalt of the basketball courts and entered the science building, which was teeming with other kids. At my locker I removed my chemistry texts and turned around, expecting to see Amelia behind me, but she wasn't there. I checked the corridor, but I couldn't see her. I didn't run into her for the rest of the day.

That evening the telephone in the kitchen rang. I was the only one who heard it. Martha, Dad's receptionist at the optometry practice, had gone home after stocking up the pantry, making us some lasagne and washing the dishes. Dad was in his study with the door closed, trying to strum along to Pink Floyd's *The Wall*. The record was loud.

I had never got into music—I didn't like how it made me feel—but Dad had never been bothered by my lack of interest. He was all for everyone doing their own thing. In any case, I figured that Dad and I actually had something in common. Dad was creative with music, and one day I would be creative with writing.

I was in my bedroom reading *Carrie* when the telephone started. I don't know how, but I knew instantly that it was Amelia calling. She had found my number in the phone book.

The ringing went on and on, until I began to feel desperate. I just wanted to be left alone. I put my book down and closed the door to my bedroom. I curled up on my Luke Skywalker doona, clutching my pillow over my head, and counted to one hundred elephants. By the time I had finished, the ringing had stopped.

I stretched out on my bed and starting reading *Carrie* again. By midnight, I had finished the novel. The girl gets her period in the high school change rooms and, in the end, destroys a whole town, going down in history as a bigger villain than the guy who assassinated J.F.K. Some other girl, Carrie's only friend, collapses and miscarries, bleeding all over the place too.

I felt like I had read something from a hidden world, and I found the experience repulsive and strangely arousing. I had a trick to calm myself down. I was pretty

flexible, and I could do this thing where I pushed my back and legs up onto the brass head of my bed so that I could watch my penis above me and, when it was time, come on my face. It was an uncomfortable position, and I wasn't entirely able to control things, so sometimes semen landed in my eyes. It stung like hell.

I cleaned up in the bathroom across the hall from Dad's bedroom, where he was sleeping alone again after Mum's weekend visit. I couldn't say that I regretted Mum being gone. The place felt safer without her. She had become alien-looking and almost impossible to ignore. I splashed cold water on my eyes and crept back to my room.

When I fell asleep I had my first nightmare about Amelia. In the dream the phone was ringing in the kitchen. It rang ever more shrilly, until I couldn't bear it anymore. I ran down the hallway to answer it, but when I picked up the receiver mounted on the wall there was only silence. As I listened to the emptiness the night in the kitchen grew until everything was dark, even the space inside my head.

I woke up in the middle of the night, terrified.

I didn't see Amelia again until the following Monday, when she showed up late for my literature class. I felt uncomfortable when I saw her—probably because of the dream. Mr Needleman wolf-whistled as she walked in, showing the pink insides of his lips beneath his bushy moustache, and winked at the class. The boys all laughed. I looked at Amelia and didn't know what to think, but I was right about the girls hating her. One of them, sitting in front of me in a football scarf, whispered 'moll' as Amelia made her way to the back row.

Not that Amelia seemed to care. She was wearing a pink baby-doll dress that barely covered her underwear. The dress had puffy sleeves that concealed her arms all the way down to her wrists, but her ample cleavage was visible, and her legs were bare. She had on white stilettos with ridiculously high heels. Her brown hair was divided into two pigtails, tied with the same pink satin ribbons as last Monday, and she had, if anything, even more make-up on her face.

She walked awkwardly towards the back of the room, and as she sat down next to me the smell of her made the air thick, as if particles of baby powder were spreading everywhere. She didn't seem to have bought any books yet, or else she had forgotten to bring them.

I reluctantly pushed *King Oedipus* towards her, and she shifted closer to me in her chair and leaned over my book. A pink ribbon and a brown pigtail, which looked unwashed, fell on the play. I could hear and feel her breathing. Out of the corner of my eye I could see the fleshy top of her breasts. Under the table her dress had ridden up so high that I could see where her legs met, just below her underpants. I could even see the crotch of her knickers, covered in pink hearts.

Oedipus was in the process of working out the horror of his situation, and Mr Needleman had asked me to read his part again. He had taken the role of the Theban who was providing Oedipus with the information that would expose the appalling truth about his wife and mother, who had caused almost as much chaos and devastation to the city as the Sphinx.

I was determined not to disgrace myself this time. I bunched my fists on the table to stop myself from typing and concentrated on the text in front of me.

As I was reading one of my lines, Amelia shifted in her seat and sat up, her pigtail and pink ribbon disappearing from my view. Beneath the table she crossed her legs and started lazily swinging one of them. Mr Needleman missed his part. When I looked up, he and Amelia were watching each other. She had a finger in her mouth. I felt sick.

Mr Needleman caught my eye. Abruptly he stood up from his desk, holding the book open in one hand and stuffing his other hand into his jeans pocket. Pacing energetically in front of the blackboard, he delivered his line. *'God! I am on the verge of saying it.'*

The other kids in the class didn't seem to have noticed anything. Under the table Amelia's bare leg kept swinging. My line was next. I concentrated on keeping my voice steady. *'And I of hearing it, but hear I must.'*

At the end of the recital, Mr Needleman briskly handed out comprehension questions, which we were to work on in pairs for the remainder of the lesson. I took the photocopied sheet without looking at him when he walked past my desk. I wasn't ready to forgive him for what had happened.

I skimmed the sheet and saw that the first two questions were 'Who was the Sphinx?' and 'What is the relationship between Oedipus's wife and Oedipus's mother?' The second question made me smile—it was clearly a trick. Mr Needleman had a good sense of humour like that.

The other kids turned to each other and started

talking—mostly about the weekend. Amelia sat back in her chair, her arms crossed over her breasts, still swinging a leg. She didn't touch her comprehension sheet. She didn't look at me, and she didn't offer a single word. Her attention was on Mr Needleman, who was sitting at his desk, focused on some marking. Seeing him lost in his work was reassuring. I wrote down my answers to the questions alone. I hunched over my work and curled my arm over the sheet, making sure that Amelia couldn't see anything.

I was surprised, after class, to find Amelia in the courtyard. She was waiting at my table when I got there. She had her back turned to me, and I thought about walking away. I didn't want to act as if I was afraid. When I sat down opposite her, placing my snack and my new Stephen King novel on the table, she casually reached over and took my banana again.

'That play is so stupid,' she said, peeling off the skin. 'As if Ear Pus or whatever his name is would find some old woman attractive, even if he didn't know it was his mum. She'd already had kids. Her vagina would have been ruined.'

She bit into the banana and started chewing with her mouth open. I left my apple untouched on the table, along with my paperback, and crossed my hands together as if I was praying. I was determined to keep myself from typing. I would not give myself away again.

As I focused on her pink lipsticked mouth Amelia started to tell me things. There was a story about a sexual escapade with a counsellor whom her mother had insisted she see. That was after Amelia had had sex with one of her mother's boyfriends. 'Mum had to go to work, I had just finished my porridge, and he bent me over the kitchen sink. God, he wanted me so bad.'

Amelia, who had finished my banana by this time, started flinging the skin from one hand to the other. 'Mum made me join the netball team on Saturday,' she said. 'She wants me to have more girlfriends.' She stopped playing with the banana skin and flung it into the bin. The top of her breasts, visible above the neckline of her dress, wobbled with the movement. There was, I saw, goose flesh there. It was another grey and cold day.

I looked up from Amelia's cleavage and accidentally met her eyes. Her eyelashes were clumped with mascara. A lank pigtail and pink satin ribbon hung on each side of her face. She looked back at me. 'There's a fundraiser at the football club this weekend. Want to come?'

I felt something close to panic. There was no way

she was going to trap me into saying anything. I looked down at the cover of *Misery* on the table. I was well into the novel. A mad woman had kidnapped a famous author, declaring herself his biggest fan, and was trying to make him do things. She wanted him to revive a female character, Misery, whom he had killed off in his last novel.

Amelia crossed her hands in front of her on the weathered boards of the table just as I had mine crossed in front of me, but I was used to ignoring teasing. I kept my eyes on the red lettering on the cover: *Misery*. It was hard to resist the urge to type the word, but I stayed strong.

'You can do that thing with your fingers if you want,' Amelia said. 'I won't tell.'

It was lucky that my mouth didn't fall open. I picked up my uneaten apple and my unread book. I left Amelia in the courtyard as the bell started to ring and was glad not to see her again for the rest of the day.

That night, after dinner, I went to my bedroom to finish *Misery*. Dad was in his study mucking around with his new electric guitar, which he had finally purchased from the music shop in town after talking about it for weeks. The amplifier was on so loud that I had to shut my bedroom door.

Martha had been and gone. She had cooked us a lamb stew with mash and peas. It was always a relief to have her come back on a Monday with several bags of fresh groceries and do some proper cooking. Martha didn't come over on the weekends, when Mum was visiting, so Dad and I had to get by on toast and baked beans. By Monday morning we had usually run out of milk and bread.

Dad had told me once that Martha was a divorcee. She was quiet and well groomed, always matching her nail polish and her lipstick. She reminded me a little of Mum who, before she got sick, used to look after herself. Martha wore heels the whole time she did the cooking and the washing up. She had put on Mum's apron the first time she had come over, but since then she had brought her own. It was white with black frills. She took it out of her handbag when she arrived with the groceries. If Dad was in his study by the time she was leaving, he'd always come out to see her off. He was a real gentleman like that.

Earlier in the year, I was coming out of my bedroom to the kitchen to get a drink when I saw them saying goodbye. They were standing on the slate tiles at the front entrance, next to Mum's aspidistra, and Martha

had given Dad a card for Valentine's Day. There was a prolonged silence as Dad opened the envelope and read the message, and then I saw him give her a twenty-dollar note for the groceries, pat her awkwardly on the bum and send her home. Afterwards, when he had retreated to his study again, I was relieved to find the card in the kitchen bin.

Martha's cooking wasn't as good as Mum's. Mum had really got into baking for a while. Looking back on it, I think she was trying to fatten us up. She never ate anything herself, and afterwards she used to do squats between washing each dish at the kitchen sink. She started to exercise strangely when she got sick.

Lying on my stomach on my bed, with *Misery* open on the pillow in front of me, I heard the phone begin to ring through the dark house. I could hear it going on and on, never rising above the noise of Dad's electric guitar but insistent all the same. I knew that it was Amelia. I buried my head under the pillow.

When the phone stopped I relaxed and went on with *Misery*. The writer in the story has just discovered that the woman holding him hostage is a serial killer. She had murdered her own father, her college roommate, various patients who had come under her nursing care and a number of babies. To get away from her the writer throws his typewriter at her head and stuffs her mouth with the pages of the manuscript she had wanted him to write—after he set them alight.

That night I had another dream. It was almost the same as the night before. The phone rang. It began to sound more and more like a siren. I ran to the kitchen to answer it. When I picked up the receiver the silence took hold and the room became pitch black.

I woke in a panic, fearing for a moment in the darkness and solitude of my bedroom that I had been buried alive.

Amelia didn't show up to literature class on Monday. I sat in the back row by myself. The air in the classroom smelled as it used to, of chalk dust and apple cores. I felt myself relax. Mr Needleman, who was wearing my favourite outfit of his—a brown leather bomber jacket over a large-collared white shirt—seemed tense.

He took the class hurriedly through the rest of the play. Oedipus's mother hangs herself because of her crimes. Oedipus unties her and takes the golden pins from her gown, stabbing his eyes as his mum's corpse

lies there in front of him. It is all too much for him to look upon—and fair enough. I felt sorry for the bloke. After all, none of it was his fault.

As Mr Needleman and I read our parts I was free to type out everything the two of us said, though I made sure I kept my hands tucked beneath the table. Then Mr Needleman handed out the essay question: 'Why is Oedipus a hero?' When he walked past my table and gave me my sheet I thought he looked a little worried, but I gave him what I hoped was a confident smile.

The class brainstormed answers for a while, with Mr Needleman writing feverishly on the blackboard. I could see the thick hair on his head moving as he wrote. At one point the chalk snapped, but he didn't join the kids in laughing. He got another piece from a box on his desk and kept going. In my literature notebook I wrote down everything that Mr Needleman scrawled on the blackboard. I tried to imitate his cramped handwriting.

After class Amelia was waiting for me again in the courtyard. I saw her back as soon as I entered the narrow passageway between the staff room and the library. She was wearing a white dress made out of a fabric that was almost see-through, and I could see her pink underpants and bra. Her hair was in a high ponytail, again tied with one of the pink ribbons. The dress was sleeveless and short, though this was the coldest day of winter so far. The fabric was ruffling like feathers in the bitter wind. Amelia's shoulders were hunched.

Amelia turned and saw me. She didn't smile. She never smiled. Her eyelids were dusted with blue eye shadow right up to her eyebrows, and mascara was smudged down her cheeks, as if she had been crying. She had on thick red lipstick. It looked like crayon.

I walked towards her with my fruit and my novel. I couldn't let her think that she had the upper hand.

'You missed a good party on Saturday night,' she said as I sat down opposite her, placing my book and fruit on my lap to make sure that she couldn't reach the banana. I bunched my hands into fists beneath the table to keep myself from typing and looked up at her, taking care not to meet her eyes.

Her dress had a plunging neckline, and I could see the swell of her breasts. I saw that she was fingering a golden crucifix, which she was wearing on a chain around her neck. The sight of her fingernails, still bitten to the quick, and the crucifix made me feel ill.

'Where did you get that?' I said. I couldn't help

myself. My voice cracked, like it used to before it broke. I had given myself away.

I started to feel frightened. Suddenly I knew that I hated Amelia more than I had ever hated anyone. I grabbed my fruit and my copy of *The Tommyknockers*—which I had moved on to after finishing *Misery*—and left the courtyard.

I didn't know where to go at first, but I had to come up with something quickly and decided on the library. I stowed my fruit inside my jumper, knowing that it was forbidden to bring food into the library, and as a precaution I stuffed my book up there as well. Then I walked through the doors and past the loans desk, without looking at the librarian, an old woman who was silently covering new books with protective plastic.

I headed to the windowless wall at the back and concealed myself at the end of a row of steel bookshelves. With my back up against the steel shelf, I stared at the white plaster of the wall. I only had to avoid Amelia for fifteen minutes: then I would be safe for the rest of the day.

The phone didn't ring that night after Martha had cooked us a fish curry, washed up and gone home. Dad had bought the new Dire Straits album, *Brothers in*

Arms, and was trying to play his electric guitar along to it in his study. The sound was loud and repetitive.

I closed my bedroom door and focused on *The Tommyknockers*. A woman finds a piece of a crashed spaceship in a field and starts to act unpredictably. Her boyfriend, a writer, is immune to the alien influence because he has a steel plate in his head. In the end, when his girlfriend starts to behave in an irrational and menacing fashion, he has no choice but to kill her.

When I finished the book Dad was still going with his guitar. He was trying to teach himself a solo, and he had the amplifier turned right up. Knowing it was safe I took off my school pants, folded them over the back of my desk chair, and got into position against my bed head. With my neck and shoulders pushed into the pillow, I started to masturbate, staring at the head of my penis above me as my hand pulled over it. My neck and shoulders began to get sore, and I couldn't manage to come.

I gave up and lay on my doona in the shape of Luke Skywalker, like I used to when I first got the bedspread. Dad was still playing his guitar. I relaxed and spread my legs. Just as I fell asleep I dreamt that the phone started to ring from the kitchen. It rang and rang until it began to sound like someone screaming.

My fear was so great that I woke up. The light in my bedroom ceiling was still on. The house was silent. Dad had gone to bed, and I was lying half naked and cold on my bed.

On Saturday morning Dad brought Mum home from the hospital again. Dad, for some reason, always rang the doorbell when they got back, and I had to let them both in. Mum stooped down at the entranceway, where I was waiting next to the aspidistra, and I give her a kiss on the cheek. Her face was covered with a fine down of hair, as if she were turning into a teenage boy, but I could always feel the blade of her cheekbone beneath her fuzzy skin. Her lips were dry, and her breath stank.

Dad, holding Mum's overnight bag, hung back until Mum went in. He was always good to her like that. Then, after he had settled her in the bedroom with her bag, Dad would give her some space. Sometimes he sat at the dining table with the weekend newspapers. That day he went into his study. Soon he started up with *Brothers in Arms* and his acoustic guitar—avoiding the electric, I think, for Mum's benefit.

I went back into my bedroom. I was ready to start work on my literature essay—I was going to hand it in early. I really wanted to impress Mr Needleman with this one. He had asked me to read in every class, and I knew that he wanted something special from me. I tried not to think about Amelia. I pretended that she didn't exist. After all, I didn't even know her real name.

I sat at my desk and went through my school bag, which was on the carpet by my feet. I removed my copy of *King Oedipus* and placed it on the desk. Next I took out my literature notebook and opened it to the relevant page. Then I laid out the pencil and eraser from my case. Last, I removed a pile of foolscap from the top drawer of my desk, knocking the paper square and placing it directly in front of me. I was ready to start writing. When I had a draft I would do the final copy on my portable typewriter, which I had moved out of the way for the time being.

I developed three arguments about King Oedipus's heroism. To begin with, I wrote, he kills the Sphinx, that evil creature who was half woman and half bird, and who had caused such bewilderment and terror among men. Oedipus answers her riddle and throws her off the cliff. By killing her, he saves not just himself but the entire kingdom.

Next, while Oedipus does marry his mother, which causes a second plague to befall the city, he does not know the horror associated with his wife, so he cannot really be held to blame.

Last, I argued, while Oedipus's mother kills herself, Oedipus never takes the easy way out. He exiles himself, going to live alone in a cave, and thereby saves the city again. After Oedipus blinds himself, so that he does not have to look upon the corpse of his wife-mother, the play gives the clear sense that everything will be okay.

I was up to the concluding paragraph when I heard a knock at the door. I turned on my swivel chair. Mum was standing there, looking tall and bony in a red terry-towelling tracksuit. Her blond hair was lank on her skull, and her blue eyes were large. Her nose was sharp as a beak. She was blocking the doorway.

'Son,' she said gently. I had almost forgotten the sound of her voice. She paused, peering toward my desk, and smiling. 'What are you up to?'

I felt like I had been caught masturbating. I turned back to my desk, pivoting on my chair. I stared at the words I had written on the sheet of paper in front of me, panic building in my ears like white noise, until I heard the bedroom door close softly behind me.

I dragged my typewriter clumsily across the desk. I took off the hard cover, scrolled some paper in and started typing. The noise of the keys clattering and the carriage returning was reassuring. Still, it took me seven goes to get the assignment right. I finished a final, error-free copy by dinner.

Dad came to get me for a late meal of beans on toast. Mum was tired, he said, and would be staying in her bedroom.

As it turned out, I didn't see Mum for the rest of the weekend. I spent Sunday in my bedroom reading another Stephen King novel, in which a car called Christine begins killing off various townspeople. When it was time for Mum to go on Sunday evening, I hid in my bedroom cupboard. I squeezed in behind two winter coats and a stack of shoeboxes, so that I would be invisible even if Dad decided to open the cupboard door.

Dad walked all over the house calling my name. I closed my eyes tight and counted one hundred elephants. When I had finished the house was quiet, and I knew that Mum had been taken away.

On Monday morning Mr Needleman wasn't in class. Amelia didn't show up again either. At first there were whispers, then the class grew noisier as we waited for the inevitable substitute. I sat alone in the back row, tuning the other kids out. I had my essay on Oedipus's heroism ready on the desk in front of me. I knew that I could hand it in when Mr Needleman returned, but I had been looking forward to giving him the paper early.

I bowed my head over the essay and stared at Mr Needleman's name and my name, which I had typed on the cover page. Under the desk I let my fingers type out our names over and over again, but my eyes began to water and the names blurred.

Mrs Orr, the principal, came in. She had coiffed silver hair and must have been close to retirement. She was known for walking around the schoolyard by herself at lunchtime, dressed fastidiously in a navy skirt and white blouse. Mrs Orr always wore red lipstick, and her eyebrows had been plucked to an arched line. While she would look benevolently at everyone, she rarely stopped to speak.

The class quietened when she entered. With everyone's attention on her, I wiped the back of my hand over my eyes.

The principal cleared her throat and smiled. She spoke slowly and with precision. 'As you may have guessed, I'll be taking your class today.' She paused. 'Would someone care to tell me which text you are studying?'

A boy in the front row held up his copy of *King Oedipus*, which Mrs Orr took, inspected for a moment and passed back. She turned to the blackboard, selected a piece of white chalk from the ledge beneath, and wrote 'Sigmund Freud' in a cursive hand, underlining it three times. Her fingernails were perfectly manicured and painted red.

'Have you already considered the significance of *The Interpretation of Dreams*?' Mrs Orr asked slowly. We all shook our heads. 'Not yet?' she said. She replaced the piece of chalk on the ledge and dusted her hands. Then she crossed them behind her back and began to pace carefully in front of the blackboard, looking at her navy shoes or the carpeted floor—it was hard to tell which.

'Sigmund Freud,' she began, 'was a famous interpreter of dreams and, on occasion, literature. His work has fallen into disrepute in recent times, but sometimes he got things right—almost despite himself, we might say.'

Two girls in front of me leaned towards each other and began whispering. I couldn't hear what they were saying, and I didn't have a clue what Mrs Orr was

talking about. I didn't bother to copy down the name of the interpreter she had written on the blackboard. I had finished my essay, after all.

'When Freud attempts to account for the dramatic power of this play,' Mrs Orr continued, 'what he ultimately suggests is that the play speaks to something dark, something hidden, within men and boys...'

Mrs Orr wasn't making any sense.

The girls in front of me were still whispering. The one with the football scarf wrapped around her neck— Donna, her name was—had called Amelia a moll under her breath a couple of weeks ago.

Mrs Orr stopped talking and pacing. With her hands still behind her back, she swivelled on her heels to face the girls. 'Yes?' she said, raising her thin eyebrows. Her red lips formed a straight line, although I could see where the lipstick had bled into the creases around her mouth.

One of the girls nudged the other. 'Is it true,' Donna asked, playing with the tasselled fringe of her scarf, 'that Mr Needleman killed himself? That he hanged himself on the stage in the school auditorium?'

I felt as if I had been punched in the stomach. I could hardly breathe.

The principal winced and looked down at her shoes. 'Mr Needleman,' she said with care, looking at us again, 'has indeed passed away.'

Most of the kids gasped, and began talking loudly. I stared at my essay. I couldn't believe what I had heard. I didn't understand how any of it could have happened. I felt tears burning behind my eyes again, and my throat felt full and heavy, like my Adam's apple was going to burst.

Then I understood: it was Amelia. She had tried to fool everyone with that baby routine, but I knew what she had done. I placed my essay on top of my pile of literature books and picked them up. I pushed my chair back and rushed out of the classroom without looking at anyone.

I went straight to the courtyard. The picnic tables were empty. The sky was grey, and the wind was freezing. I hurried to my locker in the corridor in the science wing, packed my school bag and set off for home. I counted hundreds of elephants, keeping my eyes on the footpath, as I walked down the school road and through town, passing Dad's optometry practice. When I got to our house, nestled within its neatly landscaped garden, I went to my room.

I didn't know what to do at first, but I took a pack of cards out of my desk drawer and started to play solitaire. I made sure that I handled the cards with even more precision than usual, arranging them in perfect columns, but I didn't win once in seventeen rounds.

I heard Dad come through the front door. He came straight to my room. The school had called him. He placed a glass of water and a sedative on the desk in front of me, and helped me get under my doona, still in my uniform and shoes. I closed my eyes, started counting elephants again and almost instantly fell asleep.

The nightmare, this time, was different. The phone in the kitchen was ringing urgently, like a school bell. I thought of Mr Needleman in trouble and tried to run down the hallway, but it was like moving through jelly. When I made it to the kitchen and picked up the receiver, the phone felt heavy. As usual, there was only silence, and the kitchen grew dark until I could barely see anything. That was when I knew that it was Amelia, playing her usual games.

'Why don't you say something?' I yelled. 'Why don't you tell everybody who you really are?'

Something distracted me. In the darkness I glimpsed someone slipping out of the kitchen and into the hallway.

I only saw the person's back, but I knew what I had seen. It was me, though I looked like a stranger fleeing.

I woke up feeling overheated in my clothes beneath the doona. Dad had forgotten to close the curtains, and bright afternoon sunlight was streaming through the window. It was almost blinding.

The War of the Worlds

SHE WAS lying awake, buried under her quilt, when she heard the first of the war craft shriek into the sky outside her bedroom window. She knew then that the dawn had come, though it was not yet light. There was a moratorium on launches between ten at night and six in the morning, which meant that the beginning of each day was always marked by the diabolical clamour of a take-off.

When the window stopped vibrating and the racket of the war craft began to fade away, she heard her son call out for her upon waking, as he always did. He would wait in bed until she came to fetch him, as if the floor were booby-trapped.

She switched on the bedside light, and the room instantly appeared around her, colourless and cold. A thin mist emerged with each silent exhalation from her mouth. She got out of bed, put on her dressing gown and woollen socks, and entered the empty hallway. When she pushed open her son's door it made a noise like a gunshot. She supposed it was the cold, though perhaps it had something to do with the age of the wood. Some of the bricks outside the house had come loose, crumbling onto the ground, and inside the ceilings were sagging in places from the damp.

The boy was sitting up in his bed. He had turned on his bedside light, and the walls around him were pasty and bare, except for the poster of the pale planet sticky-taped to the wall above the bed. Ares, the military scientists had called the distant world. The black space in which the planet sat was glossy from the reflection of the bedside light.

Her son, with his pale face and dark eyes, was so still and silent that it might have been someone else altogether who had been hollering. She took the boy's dressing gown from the peg on the back of the door and, when he slipped out from beneath his quilt, put the garment on him. She held his hand and led him into the kitchen, where she sat him down at the table. The fluorescent light ticked and fitted above them until it steadied into a cold glow.

She crouched down next to an old electric heater, which she had salvaged from the house across the road when the old woman living there had died. She had been lucky enough to see the crematorium truck pull up on the street outside, and she had entered the house as soon as the workers, in their plastic suits, had emerged with the body bag, heaved it into the back of the truck and driven away.

The heater worked fine despite its age and the singed smell it emitted, though with the power quotas there was no chance of leaving it on overnight. She directed the rattling machine towards the boy's legs and looked at his feet, encased in the woollen socks she had knitted, hanging beneath the table. They were so still that it was as if the socks, slightly misshapen, were on a mannequin.

She walked into the cold of the kitchen, where she poured cereal into a chipped porcelain bowl and topped it with long-life milk. She placed the dish in front of her son, gave him a plastic spoon and sat down opposite him. He began to eat, staring straight through her, as if he was caught in a dream.

Last night the boy had walked in his sleep again. She had woken to see him standing at her doorway, his hand on the blade of the doorhandle and his face the colour of a moth. The boy had been looking at her, but his eyes were vacant. Then he had sunk back into the night of the hallway, closing the door.

'What were you dreaming about last night, my love?' she asked him gently.

Under the strip light her son looked at her and opened his mouth, full of milk and pieces of cereal. The heater kept up its clatter, the hot air stirring near her legs. She frowned, and the boy closed his mouth and looked into his bowl.

She watched the boy eat and felt the quiet hovering outside the house like something solid. The peace, she knew, would be short-lived. There would be another launch soon, and then another, carrying more men away to Ares. Her father had been called into service when she was an infant. She couldn't remember anything about him. Men kept to themselves—she supposed it made it easier when it came time for them to leave for war.

The boy's father had also gone, when her son had been only weeks away from being ejected from her womb. Countless men had disappeared in the war craft specially built for the long journey. Her son had only just started at the military school, but already she could see him becoming distant.

She imagined a ship hurtling soundlessly through the blackness of space. She saw the rows and rows of men in their white suits, already induced into a coma, lining the internal walls of the war craft's chamber, ready for their violent rebirth.

Across the table she noticed that the boy had finished eating. His spoon had been abandoned in a puddle of milk in the dish, and he was looking down at it. She took the breakfast bowl and told him to get dressed for school. He could watch TV, she said, when he was ready. She ate some cereal from the same bowl, standing at the bench, then ran the tap. The water came sporadically, the pipes knocking and coughing inside the walls.

When she turned from the sink her son had reappeared. He was standing next to the table, dressed in his white uniform, already wearing his ski mask and earmuffs. She could see his mouth through another ragged cavity in the balaclava.

She walked towards her son and slowly removed the muffs. She pulled the mask, like a woollen sock,

from the boy's head and smoothed down his dark hair. She cupped his cheek, remembering how quiet he was, this dark-eyed child, even when he was born, blood-streaked and slippery. The midwife had assured her that the child was alive and well, as had her own mother, but she knew what the women were thinking. The boy was not for their world. Fingering the chunky cord trailing from her son's abdomen to the wound between her legs, she had not wanted to believe it. She still did not want to.

She took the boy's hand and led him into the living room, settling him on the decrepit sofa in front of the TV. She switched on the screen, and the light flooded her son's face. The rest of the room remained in gloom. The TV was already on the boys' channel. She couldn't remember the last time that she had watched the women's channel, but she could picture what would be on: those immaculately groomed women helping advertisers sell make-up and skin anaesthetics. Years ago she had stopped believing in it all.

She left her son fixated on the screen and walked through the dark house to her bedroom, where she pulled open the heavy curtains. Through the crusty veil of lace, which looked as if it was held together by dust, she saw that the dawn had come. There was mist floating in a band over the ground, and the long grass in their backyard was frosted stiff. The air near the window was icy on her face.

After changing into old jeans and a woollen jumper she went into her son's room, where she heaved open the drapes and switched off the bedside lamp. In the weak light she saw that the boy's pyjamas had been left on the worn mat. They lay in contorted positions as if they had been frozen, a leg broken and an arm cut off.

She looked at the black poster on the wall above the bed. In the dawn light the planet Ares appeared even more sickly. She thought of the boy's pale face hovering at her door in the dead of night. She moved towards the wall and started to pick at the sticky tape attaching each of the corners of the poster to the plaster. Then, with the thunderous noise of another war craft being launched and the pane in the window shuddering, she stood on the boy's bed and ripped the poster down. She crushed the paper as the war craft roared above the house. Holding the uneven ball, she went to the laundry, unlocked the back door and entered the foggy morning.

The sound of the ascending war craft was deafening outside. She did not look up, but it was impossible to

ignore: a blazing, steely weight above her in the raw sky. A dozen rubbish bins were nestled amid the tall grass in the narrow space between the house and the paling fence, which was leaning precipitously into the neighbour's yard. Cobwebs, stuffed between the weathered palings and suspended between long blades of grass, were laced with frost. The place looked like an old graveyard. She lifted the lid of the bin closest to the door and threw in the balled poster.

The war craft retreated into the distance overhead, growing smaller and quieter as it drew away into the pink streaks of dawn. She went back inside, locking the door behind her. In the laundry she stopped and squeezed her fingers in her fist, breathing on them. The bin lid had been so cold that her fingers felt like they had been burnt.

When she returned to the living room the boy was still watching the cartoon, his eyes wide. The action was set on a fictional planet, and the screen was pulsing with the bruised colours of an apocalyptic evening. The sound was relentless. A machine, in the rough shape of a man, had just risen from the rubble-strewn ground, bearing an enormous weapon.

She walked the boy to school under a fragile blue sky with a distant moon. The mist was thinning, and the footpath was dark and slippery. It had probably iced up overnight and melted with the dawn. She held her son's hand. The boy now wore his ski mask, and she had put on, over her woollen jumper and jeans, an old pea coat that she had found on a fossicking mission. They each had a rucksack: the boy's was a white vinyl school bag and hers was heavy-duty canvas.

There were other mothers and sons on the concrete footpath, the women made up and brightly dressed. Some clutched handbags that matched their shiny pumps. The women and boys walked in pairs, holding hands, on either side of the deserted road.

The houses along the footpaths were nearly all the same, squat and brick, with the front porches drooping. The grass everywhere was knee-high, and the dogwood trees and privet were being strangled by creepers. The houses with collapsed antennae or rubbish dumped in their gardens were the ones that had been long abandoned. Powerlines, heavy and black, connected everything in a lethargic network criss-crossing the broken asphalt of the road.

There was the rumbling of another war craft lifting

off. It might have been an earthquake—the noise of it was overwhelming. She felt the boy's hand in hers, warm and soft. She had made him, she told herself, and he was hers to hold. A blazing metallic craft rose into the sky. She squinted up at the machine screaming into the atmosphere as if the world was ending.

The war craft shrunk away, and quiet was restored. She listened to the shoes on the wet concrete: the boys' white boots, the women's high heels. It was as if nothing had happened. She might have been imagining it all.

When they arrived at the building, a brick edifice that resembled a jail, she watched the boy climb the external steel staircase to his second-floor classroom. He was part of a procession of boys in white uniforms walking up the steps through the fog. They looked like robots, she thought, except that they were clearly breathing through the mouth holes in their masks.

A boy turned at the landing at the top of the staircase and stared back at her with dark eyes. In his uniform and balaclava he could have been anyone. She waved and watched the child disappear into the building. She imagined herself bolting up the steel staircase and throwing the white-clad imposters aside, one by one, until she had identified her son.

She turned and walked away. The other mothers were forming their regular groups on the ruptured asphalt of the school parking lot, where the buses had once pulled in. Some of them might have husbands who were still around, but most would have been left behind. Their sons, like hers, were all being trained to abandon them. The women's mouths were set in precise smiles, their lipstick lustrous as their nail polish. Vapour extruded thinly from their nostrils.

She hadn't even brushed her hair, but she couldn't see how it mattered. The women would disappear when the bell clanged, and the streets would be empty of their colours and smells as if they had never been.

She pulled her coat tight and left the schoolyard. She covered the ground quickly, walking fast in the opposite direction of some women and boys who were late. The next launch, she knew, would begin soon, carrying more men away. She started to run, holding onto the shoulder straps of her empty rucksack. It was reckless to hurry on the slick concrete, but she ran faster and faster, until her lungs hurt from inhaling the icy air.

The calamitous sound of the ignition started up just as she reached the path to her mother's door. A branch from a hawthorn tree tangled in her hair. She tried to

pull away, but the thorny branch had stuck. The war craft heaved itself into the sky. It was too late. She drew closer to the tree, pressing herself into its sharp twigs. She closed her eyes and pushed her hands over her ears.

When the piercing noise began to recede she lowered her hands and stood among the tree's spiky branches, inhaling the moist smell, and remembered how its spring blossom stunk like a rotting corpse. She worked to untangle the branch from her hair and the straps of the rucksack. Looking down she saw that a thorn had pricked her thumb.

She followed the weedy brick path up to her mother's home. The ivy had grown so thick against the walls that it was impossible to tell if the house was falling apart, but the doorway had been cleared. No one came when she knocked—the doorbell, it seemed, had always been broken—but she could hear the noise of a TV inside. She hesitated, then inserted her key into the lock, closing the door silently behind her.

The TV was louder inside, and the house was warm with the smell of cooking. She knew that she shouldn't have entered; her mother had someone in the living room. There were pulses of coloured light and a steady stream of gun noise came from the door at the end of the hallway. She looked down at her sneakers and, stepping carefully on the floorboards, headed to the kitchen, where she found her mother. She had her back turned and was standing in purple stilettos at the stove, frying bacon.

A cat was sitting at her feet on the greasy floor. Its fur was as white as her mother's hair, which was dyed platinum and caught up on the back of her head in a rigid bun. The cat looked up at her with expressionless pale-blue eyes. Its tail began to move as if of its own accord. Then the cat began to lick the pink underside of a paw.

She stood at the doorway and looked at the clutter on the kitchen bench. Among the mess there was a pile of martial arts and war films, videos from another age, their plastic covers faded and cracked. Her mother had a cupboard full of them, sourced from different second-hand shops over the years. She kept them for her visitors: the aged and the infirm, those men who had no choice but to stay. The bacon, its fat blistering in the pan, was always for them too.

She said hello softly to her mother's back. The bacon spat, and her mother winced, lifting the tongs in her hand, but didn't turn around. At the same time the cat

jumped up from her mother's feet to the tacky surface of the kitchen bench, knocking over the pile of videos. One of the plastic covers, partially concealed, had a photograph of a naked woman with skin so smooth that it looked synthetic. The woman's head was cut off by the video case on top.

The cat turned in circles on the bench, and she recalled how she had, years ago in a deserted house, seen a cat restless like that before it gave birth. Queening, she remembered, was what it was called when a cat had kittens, pushing slimy parcels of life out of the stretched cavity beneath its tail. She remembered the violence of the pain she had felt when her son was born. It was as if the fabric of reality was being torn, as life, with all its vigour and brutality, forced its way into the world.

The cat finally sat down on the bench, curling its tail around its legs and staring at her intensely with its large eyes. Then it slumped on its side and closed its eyes, as if it had fallen asleep. She saw how thin the creature was beneath all its white fur. There was no way that it was carrying a litter. Lying there, next to the video cases, it looked like the pelt of a carcass.

She looked at her mother's back: at the tight yellow dress, the bulge of flesh just above the hidden bra strap. 'My son,' she imagined herself saying. 'I'm losing him.' There was the sound of crackling bacon, and an explosion sounded from the TV in the living room. She stepped away from the kitchen doorway and walked out of the house.

It was getting colder, and the mist, which had earlier looked like clearing, was closing in again. The breath she exhaled merged with the air, which was slowly thickening. She felt the fog touch upon her skin, and then it was clinging to her, cold and wet. She kept her hands stuffed in her coat pockets, but her nose and ears grew numb.

She clenched her fingers around the watch in her coat pocket. Walking into the city would take hours, but she would make sure that she was back in time to collect her son. She needed to find something for the boy—something to distract him.

The night before, preparing his meal in the kitchen, she had looked out of the window and seen him swinging around on the steel clothes hoist with its trailing lengths of wire. He had been hanging from one of the corroded limbs, still in his military school uniform, spinning around and around like a plastic doll.

The circling hoist was squealing like a creature in pain.

There was the thunder of another ignition, and the war craft tore unseen into the fog. She kept her eyes on the footpath, stepping on the cracks and weeds so that she would not lose her footing. She pictured herself falling and hitting her head, her skull caving in softly as papier-mâché. She imagined her corpse stiffening beneath the lolling powerlines as the day wore on and the war craft continued to break up the sky. At some stage there would be an anonymous call to the crematorium. When her son emerged from school there would be no one waiting for him. She saw him standing at the top of the steel staircase, the parking lot below him empty as outer space.

There was not another soul around. Now and then she saw a car in a driveway or on the roadside, its tyres deflated, rust corroding the paintwork and steel. The houses, with the heavy mist pressing down on them, could have all been uninhabited, but she knew what to look for: drapes still drawn against the morning light, foliage beginning to creep over the doorway. An open door meant that the place had already been cleaned out.

The signal for a railway crossing was flashing mutely in the fog, and a boom gate, its white paint peeling, had lowered itself over the footpath and road, blocking her passage. The alarm that should have accompanied the lights no longer worked, and she did not miss the strident clamour of it. In the cold the smell of iron and electricity was sharp.

She thought about going under the boom gate and making a run for it across the blunt lines of metal. There wasn't anyone around to stop her. She peered down the train line. The fog obscured the length of her view. It became, in the near distance, a solid wall of white.

She looked at the fences made of weathered timbers and corrugated iron that bordered the corridor of jagged rocks and iron tracks. They were dirty with old graffiti, and encroached upon by weeds and other foliage. Beyond them were the backyards of rickety homes that had been forsaken long ago and now resembled rubbish tips. Years before, she thought, the houses had turned their backs on the tracks, as though the conduit of hurtling steel might simply be ignored.

The silver locomotive shrieked out of the mist and into her view. For seconds on end it was there in front of her, hammering noise. In carriage after carriage she glimpsed men with shaved heads and white uniforms. There was row after row of them, their bodies and heads

shaking with the train's movement, as if they had a degenerative disease. There were white cords dangling from plugs wedged into their ears. The men stared blankly into the space in front of them.

A nauseating gust of air blew against her. Then the train was gone, vanishing into the mist on the other side of the tracks as if it had been sucked away. On the opposite side of the train line the ramshackle fences and their stream of graffiti returned. EAT PUSSY, she found herself reading in the vaporous silence. The letters were faded, but they had been sprayed red and stood out amid the monotonous scribble of grey paint. The signal lights in front of her continued to flash red, the two of them taking it in turns.

The train, she knew, was on its way to the airbase, from which the men would be launched into the heavens, kitted out for war. She thought of the poster of Ares crushed in the bin at the side of the house and felt a deep quietness that brought to mind a stone well.

The lights stopped pulsing, and the boom gates returned to their vertical positions. She stuffed her hands into her coat pockets and headed off.

The mist became sparser as she neared town. The houses were packed together and wedged against the footpath. There was less greenery, and the concrete footpath, while undulating and cracked, was not as disturbed by weeds. The bitumen road broadened out but was dotted with street signs and traffic lights, some on poles stuck in concrete islands, others suspended from power lines. The noise of the ascending war craft, unseen in the mist, filled the streets.

She began to pass the shops, their windows long since broken—even between the iron bars—and their doors gaping. The shelves inside had been toppled, and the floors and escalators were strewn with inert rubbish.

She passed the hospital and the vacant hulk of its ambulance bay. Next door was a stone church, its towering copper steeple matching the elevation of the high rises. She had been inside the building once and seen the enormous effigy of the church's saviour on the back wall: a man, cut from white marble and nailed to a lofty cross. There was a smaller statue of a woman in the antechamber, as though she had been left behind.

She stopped suddenly on the path outside an empty service station, recognising a crematorium truck on the opposite side of the road. She could hardly believe her luck. Its engine was silent, the high cabin unoccupied. She looked around the deserted streets, then gripped

the straps of her rucksack and bolted across the foggy road, her sneakers slapping the wet asphalt.

Leaping the concrete traffic island, she ran straight past the truck and did not stop until her hands hit the glass door to the foyer of the building. A heavy chill pressed against her face and chest as she entered the dim room. She paused, saw the access to the stairs next to the lift and headed quickly towards it. She entered the night of the stairwell, closing the door quietly behind her.

The stairwell was icy, and despite the cold there was the unmistakeable stink of something rotting. The only light came from a fluorescent exit sign over her head. The smell of decay, and the cold air, seemed to be emanating from the basement. The stairs heading there descended into pitch black. She leaned on the back of the door to catch her breath. Sweat was trickling down the skin beneath her jumper and the rucksack.

She heard the hidden work of the lift's engine and pulleys inside the wall next to her. The lift doors quaked open, and she held her breath. There were firm footsteps in the tiled foyer. She imagined the figures in white plastic carrying out the slumped body. Then she heard the truck's engine start. The uproar of a war craft added its din. After a time, there was silence.

She emerged from the stairwell into the gloomy foyer. The mist was pressing against the glass doors of the building. The street, with its broken asphalt and scattering of traffic lights, looked barren. She turned and pressed the button for the lift. The steel doors provided a dull mirror: she saw herself waiting nervously in her shabby jeans and jumper, the shoulders of her pea coat crossed by the straps of her empty rucksack.

The room behind her was small and drab, with a solitary sofa pressed against the far wall. The vinyl of the seats was ripped, and the springs looked like they had collapsed.

She raised her eyes to the arch of numbers and letters on the narrow strip of wall above the lift. A swivelling arrow, like the hand on a clock face, seemed to be stuck on Ten. The lift, for whatever reason, was not coming down.

Even if she took to the stairs, she had no idea how to find the room vacated by the dead person. There would be nothing to offer her son. When she got home she would have to retrieve the poster of Ares from the bin and smooth it back onto the wall above the boy's bed.

She looked at her muddy image in the lift doors

and stepped closer, so that she was standing at the seam where they met.

She remembered her interrupted night and felt exhausted. Perhaps she might fall asleep on her feet, she thought, hanging onto the straps of her bag. She closed her eyes and saw the boy sleeping beneath his pasty quilt, the ghostly planet above him almost lost in its sea of black. The light of the clock radio on his bedside table spilled green over him. Then he was sitting up emitting a high-pitched scream, like a kettle boiling on the stove.

She heard the doors shuddering and opened her eyes. There was no lift in front of her. She looked down at her feet. She was standing on the threshold of the lift shaft, which was black and empty, an abyss.

II

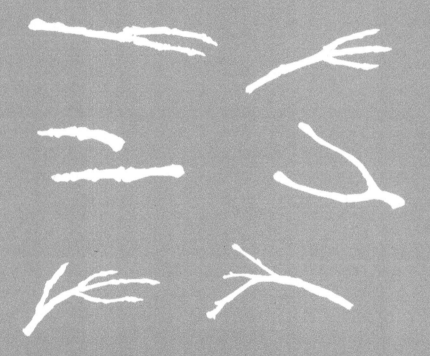

A Roānkin Philosophy of Poetry

I WORKED for a while with the second cousin of an acquaintance of the notorious Minean nationalist poet Honoré Tutkanen, whose book *The Overall Underling* had done little, my colleague and I agreed, to advance sympathy for the pig breeder. This colleague, a lecturer in the faculty of business and law, had initiated an ambivalent friendship with me when he connected the name on my pigeonhole with a controversial sonnet on the Ugrilian practice of bovine circumcision. I had been fortunate to have the poem published in *Moth*, a journal widely regarded in an especially small circle.

On the few occasions I saw the colleague in the staff room during my nine years as a PhD student and

casual tutor in creative writing, he regularly referred to a peculiarly sensitive tome written by the little-known Cronkian anthropologist Zed Roānkin, who had moonlighted in his time as a dogsled driver. Roānkin's book was about an extinct people whose winters were spent under the oneiric flashes of the northern lights, and whose customs and language were distinguished by a charming mixture of bluntness and ambiguity. Their theory of poetry, my bearded colleague in business and law promised, was sure to be of interest to me. Unfortunately the good fellow was, for a prolonged period of time, unable to produce the actual volume, a library book that he had apparently misplaced.

One day at the frenetic start of an academic year, as I adjusted to an unprecedentedly strenuous teaching workload of two creative writing workshops a week— while also continuing my struggle against the writer's block that had impeded progress on my thesis for eight years—I discovered the book in my pigeonhole. It was a handwritten ten-page stapled A5 pamphlet. It had been delivered along with a more conventional volume called *Workplace Fraud*.

There was a note from my hirsute colleague, who wrote that he had retired to dedicate his life to the

Morgonites, rumoured by some to be a ruthless economic rationalist organisation. The note also revealed that my former colleague had come across Zed Roānkin's pamphlet—and the other book—while cleaning out the bottom drawer of a filing cabinet, which was filled with reams of notes taken at various annual meetings of the faculty of business and law over his indubitably busy career. It would be appreciated, he wrote, if I would return both items to the community library upon completing my examination of them, taking care of any associated overdue fines.

I will not report here everything that Roānkin wrote in that excellent book, for I would be merely producing an unequal replica of a study not especially concerned with my particular field of expertise. However, of unusual interest to me, as my former colleague had predicted, was the final, brief but consequential chapter on aesthetics and, within that chapter, the penultimate subsection, on poetry. As a preface to my comments on these concluding parts, suffice it to say that Roānkin called the extinct northern ethnic group the Roānkins because they did not, as far as Roānkin could solicit with his limited Roānkin vocabulary, have a name for themselves. Roānkin also described the Roānkins

as living in harmony with the catastrophic winters that took up an interminable part of each year of their existence until they all died.

In the chapter outlining their theory of art, Roānkin writes that the Roānkins believed that art should deal only with the superficial realities of day-to-day living. More extraordinarily, Roānkin claims that the Roānkins believed art to know nothing of the abyss. They did concede, however, that art could certainly imagine the terrifying death to be met by one unlucky enough to fall into an icy crevasse while being chased by a bear awoken early from its winter sleep.

The subsection on poetry begins by demonstrating the astonishing economy—the charming bluntness and ambiguity, as my old colleague put it—of the language of the Roānkins, in which single verbs can denote multiple complex activities. For instance, the verb for composing a poem and playing with one's faeces are the same.

I must confess that at this point in my original reading—which occurred clandestinely, during a poetry workshop in which I had set the students an exercise in defamiliarising a warthog—I experienced a moment of scepticism. I suspected that Roānkin, like many a scientist, might be hostile to literature and that this antagonism may have skewed the objectivity of his data. Perhaps I allowed myself also to question the goodwill of my former colleague in business and law in passing on the Roānkin treatise to me.

I had a precedent for such qualms. My mother and father, who worked respectively as a superannuation officer and a business analyst, had made clear their hesitations about my professional interest in poetry. In fact, when I announced to them at the age of thirty-two that I had received a calling to undertake a part-time postgraduate degree in verse composition they evicted me from the family home. It was fortunate that an ex-girlfriend from my secondary school years, by then a single mother of seven, permitted me to move into a shed located in the backyard of her rented house. The garden shed abutted a homely chicken coop, and I had been living there comfortably, beneath a picturesque series of power lines, ever since.

Sitting in the classroom that auspicious day, after succumbing very briefly to uncertainty, I was persuaded by the final lines of Roānkin's book that the findings of this valiant study of the vanished northern people named after its honourable investigator were unquestionably true. Roānkin's last words outlining the Roānkins' philosophy of poetry sung on the page like a plague of locusts granted only twenty-four hours to copulate before they die. Yes, Roānkin or the Roānkins spoke to me thus, even though, I concede, they would never have known of such creatures in the cold familiarity of their white world.

After re-reading Roānkin's sensitively worded translation of the Roānkins' philosophy of poetry—and surreptitiously placing it, along with *Workplace Fraud*, in the community library's after-hours returns chute—I found myself, night after mysterious night, dreaming of the strange hair of pigs and of Zed Roānkin. Soon after, I experienced what I could only describe as an insomniac week of night trances that broke my debilitating case of writer's block.

Lying on my back on my foldout cot, listening to the restless chickens in the coop outside and contemplating the dark corrugations of the shed roof above me, I found that poems emerged fully formed in my mind. I turned on my torch and began to write them down. During those inspired nights, sitting on my cot next to a push mower and a rusty collection of gardening tools,

I transcribed a series of poems on the variegated forms of Bodeal flax and the wormy blackness of earth.

That sequence of verse came to constitute the creative component of my PhD thesis. While my assessors seemed to have trouble fully appreciating the work, the manuscript was nevertheless passed without issue and swiftly published by Inveigle, a small poetry press that I established with the financial support of an emerging writer's grant. I was particularly proud of the company logo, which I designed myself without assistance. It was the bold outline of the face of a man, featureless except for a large moustache, which I imagined had distinguished the visage of Zed Roānkin.

I attribute the tenure I secured after completing my PhD to the publication of my poetry manuscript, which I had called *Dabbling in the Dirt*. Similarly, I accredit the research leave subsequently bestowed upon me to the favourable review of that chapbook posted on the blog of Liberty Quan, whose material person could be found in an unfamiliar suburb of the faraway city of Barcøl Tur. (I had used the internet to sell copies, one of which had been purchased by that unknown but generous amateur vegetable harvester.) This period of leave granted by my institution was of personal and

professional significance: it enabled me to search for the dogsled driver who had transported me to such heights. It allowed me to search for Zed Roānkin.

In order to plan my quest I went to retrieve Roānkin's pamphlet from the community library. I eventually located it with the assistance of an eccentric librarian, an old woman who acted more like a co-conspirator than a rational custodian of books. She led me to the economics section, where the volume was surprisingly catalogued between *Tricks to Retiring Peacefully* and another title that I happily recognised: *Workplace Fraud.*

Upon escaping the peculiar librarian and reacquainting myself with the contents of the A5 booklet, I decided upon the brief period of the northern summer for my solo re-creation of Roānkin's epic journey from his homeland to the realm once inhabited by the Roānkins. I regretted that my expedition would be less authentic for travelling in milder conditions, but I had become, over the course of my otherwise pleasant years in a garden shed, sensitive to the cold.

Having mapped a viable route for my quest, I soon found myself riding on the back of a mule along a gravel roadside in the uppermost province of Fermine, in Cronk. My head was protected by a contraption identified, I believe, as a *húttu-hátti* by the introverted mule-rental operator, who charged me an exorbitant twenty-seven solanges for the mule and hat despite my stated interest in an eminent compatriot of his. This hat protected me not from the heat of the sun, which was unexpectedly considerable, but from the swarms of mosquitoes that plagued the marshlands of the northern regions of Cronk during this time of year. The insects hovered over my faithful mule and me like a living silhouette, the two of us granted a reprieve only when occasional fast-moving cars stirred the air in passing.

I met not a soul on those first days travelling across the interminable marshlands, although reindeer became ever more plentiful. When the sun hung low and the light started to fade in a sky electric with mosquitoes, I would set up camp with my mule on the gravel of the roadsides, where it was dry. The nights—such as they were in this perplexing place—lasted only hours before the region's birds began their raucous darting through the mosquitoes. I believe that I had truly begun to understand the desperation and despair Roānkin must have experienced in order to realise the territory of the seemingly mythical Roānkins.

Mid-morning of my third day on mule-back I arrived at the unremarkable village of Ostenich, which I estimated to be some distance further north from my starting point in Fermine. I tied my mule to a bicycle rack outside the Old Ostenich Inn, which I had seen announced by a neon sign, and walked through a herd of mangy reindeer milling in the car park outside the public house. Upon making my entrance I advanced immediately on the only fellow in the place, an ancient bearded man residing at a burgundy-coloured table in a dark corner. He was unfamiliar with my language, but when I showed him the pamphlet by Zed Roānkin—for I had it stowed in my shirt, against my chest—and a brown ten-solange bill, he became extraordinarily animated, displaying a thick tongue and poor habits in dental hygiene.

I cannot relate here everything that this unusually loquacious native of Cronk said, for he spoke a language unknown to me. However, I can confirm that he verified that his compatriot Roānkin, precisely as I imagined, had passed this way, that he had a bushy handlebar moustache, and that he had travelled through vast expanses of snow with a pack of dogs which smelled more rankly than him. This last detail the old man communicated through a series of energetic yet simple gestures.

A Roānkin Philosophy of Poetry

When my narrator, whose name I had been unable to fathom, retreated to a mirrored bar to purchase himself a refreshment—I was a teetotaller, poetry being my intoxicant—I heard a peal of laughter. It struck me how grounded yet surprising these people were. Indeed, their paradoxical qualities were such that I wondered if they were not only compatriots of Roānkin but also descendants of the vanished Roānkins. I could feel my heart pounding in my chest, and I knew that I could not help but write a poem about this place.

When I began thinking about what I knew would be my opus magnum on Roānkin and the Roānkins, a work which would far surpass *Dabbling in the Dirt* in its grappling with the earthly and unearthly nature of the earth, I held in mind the epics of the ancient Zarmqué—which sing of the seasonal assault of crickets and of horses trapped in fishing nets—as well as the bons mots of the monk known to history only as Gorbes. The rhythm of the mule, as it lumbered along the gravel verge in the glooming swamp, convulsing its head to relieve itself of the relentless insects, enhanced my poetic reflections.

I decided to continue on my pilgrimage along the highway for one more night, before retracing my route in order to return the mule to the taciturn mule-rental operator, as agreed, by the end of seven days. I knew it was unlikely that I would find any further trace of the Roānkins in this short time. In any case, I believed that I was almost ready to begin writing. By the ambiguous light of nightfall, after I had zipped up my swag to the sound of mosquitoes and the four-legged beast's quivering, I had the most uncanny dreams.

I dreamt that I was Roānkin lying among the stink of his sled dogs, the fur around their mouths stained with the blood of hares shot for their supper, and then I dreamt that I was one of the Roānkins, moving quietly upon Roānkin as he slept among his dogs in the snow. I looked at the tenebrous flesh of his closed eyelids, at the ice beginning to encrust his heavy moustache and at the notepad nestled among the anthropologist's reeking furs. I knew that the philosophy of poetry scribbled down somewhere on those pages was mine.

Roānkin and the Judge of the Poetry Competition

IT WAS when I was judging the Hermet Brethren Nature Lovers' Poetry Prize, reciting lyric poem after lyric poem to myself, as was my habit when judging verse, that I discovered the poem that was to be my ruin. Among the 1523 hymns to elegant seabirds and noble waterfowl that had been presented to me by the competition administrators, I discovered a wretched concrete poem. It was in the shape of the externalised testes of a land mammal.

The poem was aggressively phrased and referred to a miscellany of perverse phenomena: a form of surgery practised on the males of species, including human beings; the high pitched whine of a bagless vacuum cleaner; and an artificially produced and sterile zonkey—a stupid and morose animal by the poem's account. It ended with some remedial recommendations, listing the names and screening times of various television nature documentaries.

The poem was numbered 973 in the dilapidated box of anonymous entries that the administrators had sent me. It was called 'Eunuch', and it was dedicated to one whose name was foreign to me but who continues to plague both my dreams and my waking life. The dedication read: *For Zed Roānkin.*

As I sat at the leather-topped mahogany desk in my study with the A4 sheet in my hands, my voice abruptly silenced, the concrete poem at first provoked little more than distaste. However, my repugnance quickly grew to anger.

To begin with, the poem was an affront to Hermet Brethren, the agoraphobic monk and nature poet in whose memory the prize had been named. He had written such classic examples of nature verse as 'The Delicate Legs of the Great Loon' and 'The Greater Charms of the Lesser Flamingo', before passing away during an afternoon nap in his sequestered lodgings. The reprobate poem was also an offence to the competition's chief administrator, Lester Pyker, who had raised an unprecedented reward of one hundred bols plus a blind artist's watercolour of a blue crane.

In fact, the concrete poem was nothing less than an insult to lyric poetry, to which I had dedicated my life, one might say, forgoing marriage, children, household pets and standard forms of employment. For thirty years I had edited the poetry annual *Nature's Hush*—with the assistance of an ongoing and generous bequest from a regular contributor—honouring the well-crafted verse hymn to the natural world.

Poetry, I had always believed, should be a gift from one soul to another. It should be sung aloud to the sea, soaring on its own wings. A good nature poem should allow the poet—and the reader—to transcend his or her body. Bird poems, of course, were the most appropriate vehicles for such flights from one's corporeal being. Indeed, this was precisely what I had opined in my recent editorial to the thirtieth anniversary issue of *Nature's Hush*, which I had just sent out to its 179 contributors, along with a note advertising the availability of additional copies for the special sum of thirty bols.

The antique cuckoo clock on the study wall began to sound the hour—it was midday—and I realised that I was hungry. Being generally preoccupied with my ineffable calling, I was hardly a gastronome and, in truth, rarely went to the effort of purchasing food. However, it had been hours since I had breakfasted on devilled ham and cucumber in the kitchen of my retired neighbour, Edda Vôle.

The old woman was a migrant whose skills in my language were rudimentary but whose talents in the kitchen were generally agreeable. She had recently moved into the flat across the driveway and regularly received visits from me at mealtimes. I would bring back issues of *Nature's Hush*, which I would read from as Edda silently and brusquely divided up her repast to share with me. While her tangle of long grey hair made it hard to see her face, I had the sense that she benefited most from the poems about simpler waterbirds, such as ducks and geese, which I recited to her with what I hoped was edifying gentility.

On the tenth call of the cuckoo clock, though, my appetite for lunch disappeared. It was then, as I sat surrounded by shelves lined with pristine editions of *Nature's Hush*, that the concrete poem in my hands struck me as an imposter. It was surely a hoax.

I thought of the swindle uncovered by the literary critic Mang Fang, who had, in a shocking photographic exposé in the *Real News*, outed the author of the prize-winning poem 'Ode to the Dusky Moorhen' as a chimpanzee. The primate, it appeared, had acquired a taste for the eggs of that bird, and thus a refined appreciation of its behaviour and habitat. The poem was widely regarded as a coarse choice for the Winz Lootinen Nature Lovers' Poetry Competition, and following the revelation of the hoax, the adjudicator, Graine Easter, was ostracised. Once a budding poet— although, I hasten to add, his vulgar nature poems were never published in *Nature's Hush*—Easter fled to the mountains of Boan, where he took up work as a yodelling goatherd.

There was no chance, of course, of my making such a mistake. I balled up the offending poem and threw the paper into the wastepaper basket by my desk. Then, determined not to let the fraud disturb my routine, I extracted more entries from the large cardboard box on the floor next to me. I cleared my throat and resumed reciting the bird poems in my customary delivery. The advancing years had certainly not wearied my delicate timbre. Then I assigned the poems to the appropriate piles on my desk—'no', 'maybe', 'yes'—each already hundreds of A4 pages deep.

However, as I chanted lyric poem after lyric poem, I had to concede that the concrete poem had unsettled me. The poems honouring the timeless grace of the tern and the ibis, despite my sensitive performances, ultimately refused to soar. Finally, my voice cracked. I felt confused and, remembering the sterile zonkey in the concrete poem, absurdly depressed.

In an attempt to reinvigorate myself, I recalled the recent event held in honour of the thirtieth year of *Nature's Hush*. It had been a glorious occasion, which I had hosted in my neighbour's flat, utilising her catering skills—though the recently retired widow protested that she had only ever worked professionally as a construction worker.

I remembered how I had, in an endearing moment, caught the squat-figured old woman watching me and my distinguished peers from the doorway of her kitchen. Her face was impassive—momentarily, almost hostile—but I had long suspected that she was fascinated by my numinous vocation. And I remembered how Raul Kart's fluty and, at times, whispered reading of 'The

Mute Swan in Fog' during the entree of dried chicken feet prompted many diners to lay down their cutlery to listen more attentively. Then I remembered how, later that night, the chicken feet had proved disagreeable.

Staring at my mahogany desk, I decided that it was time for a drink. I did not return to the judging that afternoon. Instead, ensconced in a reclining chair in my sitting room, I consumed an entire bottle of Nünn's cream whisky liqueur, a gift from my wealthy benefactor. I had decided, through whatever means necessary, to wipe the poem called 'Eunuch' from my mind. Eventually I fell asleep on the leather seat, only to suffer a night of distastefully violent and erotic dreams in which a chimpanzee slipped soft egg after soft egg into his gummy mouth.

Before dawn I spoke the name of Roānkin into the darkness, as if in a malevolent trance. Only then did I wake up, my crotch throbbing and my body damp with sweat. Somewhere in the sitting room an unseen mosquito was lamenting.

It was before daybreak but I got up, switched on the lights and had a hot shower. I resolved to put the concrete poem behind me. With a pair of tongs I retrieved the odious piece of verse from the wastepaper basket in my study and carried it into the kitchen. I opened the doors to the empty cupboards, looking in vain for some matches. The poem had to be dispensed with. I clasped the A4 page under running water at the sink until the paper was so soggy that it began to fall apart. Then I used the tongs to stuff the pulp through the cavities in the drain.

Upon returning to my study I began to feel seedy— whether from the effects of the creamy alcohol that I had consumed the night before or the poem I could not be sure. The light from my desk lamp had an unfortunate green tinge. I poured the box of remaining entries onto the leather top of my desk, randomly selecting the last as the winner, despite the back of the paper being stained by rodent excrement and the dusty corpses of silverfish. When I turned the page, I saw that it was titled, regrettably, 'Elegy for the Elegant Egret'.

The weeks after the Hermet Brethren Nature Lovers' Poetry Prize saw the full extent of my crisis materialise. Disturbed by nightmares about sterile zonkeys and waking repeatedly with Zed Roānkin's name on my lips, I remembered the concrete poem's curative suggestions.

I began watching late-night nature documentaries on television, a machine I had hitherto kept stored in a closet in case of national emergency.

I was appalled by what I witnessed. Green snakes were fornicating in writhing tangles in the rainforests of Ngui. There were vultures, suffering from kidney failure and visceral gout, nearing extinction in the deserts of Molfart and Zound. Prostheses were being crafted for cows that had lost legs to frostbite in the highlands of Wöll. In the swamps of Drømland, in Potonk, human beings were dying from licking diabolical toxins excreted by the glands of cane toads.

It seemed that nature, in the aftermath of the concrete poem, had been thrown into abject chaos. Even my own body had become unfamiliar: vulnerable to awkward bouts of arousal, prone to the ejection of unpleasant noises, perspiring and malodorous.

Nevertheless, each morning I showered and valiantly attempted to continue work on the thirty-first issue of *Nature's Hush*. I collected the submissions from my letterbox downstairs, but once I had the envelopes open on my desk the poems celebrating the refined heron or the superior auklet proved powerless to lift my despairing soul. When I tried to recite them in my finest manner, my throat would spasm and my body would be wracked by coughing fits.

In the end I let the reams of A4 sheets accumulate, unsorted, on my desk. When they began to spill onto the floor, I stooped down and stuffed the pages into the gaps on the bookshelves. I still believed, in those days, that the gift of poetry appreciation might return to me.

That was before the unfortunate morning on which I undertook my daily excursion to the letterbox outside in my dressing gown and found it necessary to flee my elderly neighbour as she returned from the supermarket laden with groceries. Edda Vôle, walking along the footpath, looked nothing short of incensed. I ran back into my flat and shut myself in my study, where I sat in my usual morose condition, surrounded by the lyric poems amassing around the room.

Suddenly claustrophobic, I pulled open the blinds above my desk, snapping the cord and exposing myself to the world. On the top railing of the weathered fence outside my window, two glistening skinks had attached themselves to one another. Further along, a cat was sitting on a bin, worrying at a disembowelled mouse.

I pulled at the blinds in a desperate bid to protect myself, but I only managed to haul the aluminium strips onto my desk. I turned to the familiar cuckoo clock ticking on my study wall. It began to sound, the old wooden bird thrusting lewdly forth. It was then I knew I was having a breakdown.

That day I abandoned my study. I let the poetry submissions accumulate in the letterbox, along with other correspondence, including cheques from my benefactor and household bills. I spent my days, as well as nights, on the leather sofa in front of the television in my dressing gown, compulsively watching the vulgar nature documentaries recommended by the concrete poem. I stayed there even after the electricity had been turned off, staring at my reflection in the grey bulge of the screen. As a result of weeks with little nourishment, I had become gaunt and almost grotesque.

There were times when I rallied and determined to find the identity of the poet who had ruined my life, having hopelessly confused that anonymous author with the dedicatee Roānkin, whose name had been impressed indelibly upon me. I speculated that Roānkin might be a resentful author whose work I had rejected for publication in *Nature's Hush*. Alternatively, he might be an academic, such intellectuals being renowned for their bitterness towards the fine arts.

One night I resolved to attend a poetry recitation at the local hall and enquire if the audience could help me with my quest. I had not attended a poetry event for some time. My physical condition had deteriorated so far that, during the loftiest moments of a reading, like a sufferer of Turkette's syndrome, my body would experience an irrepressible compulsion to expel something obscene.

But on this occasion I contained myself until the open microphone session, when I rose from my chair at the back of the room and took to the stage. I asked the gathering of seven if any of them had heard of a man named Zed Roānkin. The room fell silent. I am not sure, to this day, if it was the name of Roānkin that stunned them or my dishevelled state. The water supply to my flat, by that time, had been cut off.

It is true that Roānkin had so fully preoccupied my thoughts that, for a long time, I neglected to consider the real and anonymous author of the concrete poem. However, many months after judging the Hermet Brethren Nature Lovers' Poetry Prize, I finally recovered my wits sufficiently to call the chief administrator of the competition.

First I enjoyed an excellent dinner of crumbed venison, which my elderly neighbour retrieved from her refrigerator upon my impromptu visit to her flat. Then in a telephone conversation carried out from the widow's bedroom—my phone had long been disconnected—I requested the identity of the author of competition entry number 973.

I am ashamed to admit that, in explaining my current condition to Lester Pyker, who was not only the competition overseer but also an old friend, I started to weep. As I did so, Edda switched on the kitchen radio—a sensitive gesture—so that the sound of a castrato singing a requiem became indistinguishable from my own crying. On the other end of the line, Pyker cleared his throat, conceded that I had made an unusually morbid choice in the winning bird poem, and asked me to hold while he looked up the author of the concrete poem.

As I was waiting, sitting on Edda Vôle's double bed, with its unusual zebra-patterned bedspread, I dried my eyes and looked around the room of this simple woman who had provided me with so many meals. On the bedside table was a television guide, in which the old widow had highlighted the titles of a number of nature documentaries.

I stood from the bed, picking up the telephone, and

almost tripped on the cord of a bagless vacuum cleaner, which had been left plugged in.

I carried the telephone, the receiver still at my ear, to a dressing table at the far end of the room on which I could see a modest pile of books. Beneath a library book entitled *Tricks to Retiring Peacefully* was a thin and grubby pamphlet, also from the local library, called *A Roānkin Philosophy of Poetry*. I grabbed at it. The handwritten pages revealed an earthy and vigorous philosophy of verse that was utterly foreign to me.

As I replaced the pamphlet on the dresser I spotted the decorative knife—an exotic souvenir from Edda's homeland, by the looks of it—poised beside the pile of books. I looked into the mirror and cupped my crotch. I saw that the poem called 'Eunuch', allegedly for Zed Roānkin, was intended for none other than me.

Roānkin and the Research Assistant

I FIRST heard the name of Zed Roānkin when I was working for the inestimable Professor Nûte Bërger at the University of Harvikoski. I had recently completed a part-time Master's thesis on children's haiku, while working as an assistant at the university creche, and found myself fantasising about the astonishing possibility of an academic career—something I had once believed would be forever beyond my reach.

At the same time Professor Bërger, a renowned practitioner of epically sized poetry installations and the foremost expert on the Bërger School of monumental poetics, was given a personal chair by my university and assigned the task of reinvigorating the poetry department. He immediately advertised for a research assistant. I submitted an application, hardly believing my luck.

At his previous institution Professor Bërger had been successful in procuring numerous sizeable grants, including one to translate his monographs on the Bërger School into seventeen languages and another to pressure clean his poetry monuments. I regret to say that I had never seen these installations, which had been commissioned for the abandoned northern suburbs of Lümp following the nuclear emergency there. Still, I knew of the professor's illustrious reputation.

When I received email notification that my application to be his research assistant had been successful, I was as excited as a teenager—as my mother said, with typically dour concern, when I called her with the news. She was a practical woman who, to my regret, lacked the capacity to appreciate my academic vocation. As a single mother of twelve, she was of the firm belief that the child-care industry offered more prospects.

The position of research assistant, as advertised, would involve a total of ten hours of work, but I gave up my job at the creche to fully dedicate myself to whatever tasks Professor Bërger might have in mind for me. I imagined working collaboratively with the professor on his next monumental poetry installation, networking by his side at Bërger School poetry conferences, and co-authoring academic papers for publication.

Settling myself into the stationery room in the faculty basement, which had been assigned to me as my office, I received an email from the professor's postdoctoral research fellow, a woman named Arda Gwin, instructing me that my job would be to organise a symposium. It was to be called The Bërger School of Monumental Poetics, and Professor Nûte Bërger would be the keynote—and only—speaker.

Dr Gwin's email listed the names of ninety-three academics who should be invited to attend. Their airfares and accommodation would be covered. However, as Professor Bërger's professorial allowance did not extend to catering, Dr Gwin's email explained, I would be required to supply morning tea: freshly brewed coffee and, ideally, an assortment of jam-filled pastries.

I could hardly believe my good fortune in being given the opportunity to assist Professor Bërger with his esteemed research. Even my office seemed incredibly propitious. Being located in a stationery room would definitely be an advantage in the event of network failure.

I also found that the isolation and lack of natural light, far from being an inconvenience, inspired me to work well into the nights. And, while I was only being paid for ten hours of work, I was more than happy to put in extra time to ensure that the event honouring Professor Bërger was a success.

On the day of the symposium I collected eighteen visiting scholars from the Harvikoski airport and transported them to the lecture theatre, Professor Bërger's meagre budget being insufficient to cover the cost of taxi fares. Three at a time the guests clambered into the back of my rusty two-door automobile, while the others patiently awaited my return trips despite their international reputations and the poor coffee at the airport cafeteria.

By the time I had finished collecting the professor's guests my car's engine was rattling but, more importantly, the lecture theatre contained a dozen and a half exceptional men. I served them coffee, which I made to order using a machine I had hired for the occasion, and a range of home-made pastries. I also met the stylish Arda Gwin, who was in attendance to greet the professor's guests and who was kind enough to point out to me, with a perfectly manicured finger, any soiled crockery or food scraps abandoned on seats or in the aisles.

At last, Dr Gwin took to the stage and informed the audience of Professor Nûte Bërger's imminent arrival. I was able to sit down, next to the refreshments at the back of the auditorium, and anticipate meeting my distinguished employer. When the professor entered the stage, kissing Arda Gwin on the hand and gallantly inviting a round of applause for her hospitality, I saw that he was surprisingly slight of stature. He wore tight brown pants and walked with a noticeably light step. I thought briefly of my father, an unsuccessful jockey who had left my mother when I was sixteen. However, when Professor Bërger began the slideshow of his impressively sized polyhedral text-lettering-and-graffiti clusters in Lümp—encrusted with radioactive scum though they were—he exuded triumph. I am afraid to say that I fell instantly in love.

At the end of two hours and thirty-four minutes, the professor took a drink from the bottle of mineral water that I had placed on the lectern and nodded to Dr Gwin, who walked onto the stage in her smart skirt and called for questions. After various erudite and fascinating soliloquies from each of the learned men in the audience, a middle-aged and stout woman, whom I had certainly not invited to the conference, put up her arm.

She reminded me of my mother, a stern woman who had not only raised a dozen children alone but forged a career in animal midwifery, establishing regular arrangements with a number of champion alpaca breeders. I remembered my mother's blunt response when I decided to embark on the postgraduate study of children's haiku—although she did concede the value of succinct forms of childhood expression—and I panicked: I should have been more vigilant in monitoring entry to the auditorium.

The sturdy-looking woman stood in the midst of the audience of men and introduced herself as the faculty cleaner. She explained that she had learned about poetry unexpectedly one day in the community library, while locating a book called *Workplace Fraud*. Was Professor Bërger, she asked—with more than a hint of aggression—familiar with the Roānkin philosophy of poetry?

I held my breath. I had never heard of this Roānkin. Professor Bërger gave the woman in the audience his most winning smile. Then he raised his eyebrows at

Dr Gwin on the stage next to him. She called an end to questions, and the proceedings wrapped up swiftly. Arda Gwin had saved the day. I could have wept with gratitude.

The professor was besieged by scholars after the event and left, alongside Dr Gwin, before I could be introduced to him. Yet I was far from disappointed. As I held the door open for the departing guests and then tidied the empty room, I was trembling with relief that I—and the woman I had inadvertently permitted to enter the lecture theatre—had not ruined the professor's symposium.

I scrubbed jam from the auditorium seats, and packed the hired crockery and coffee machine into boxes. Then, after returning several carloads of academics to the airport—I found them milling around on the street outside the auditorium—I drove to the service station to refuel for the final time that day. As I stood inhaling petrol fumes I was no longer worrying about the woman who had mentioned Roānkin, or about the diminishing credit on my card. I thought only of Nûte Bërger's slender thighs and generously proportioned poetry clusters.

After completing an additional task assigned by Dr Gwin—mailing out 126 review copies of the latest translation of one of the professor's monographs, purchasing stamps with the remaining credit on my card—my work as the professor's research assistant came to an end. I discovered that the basement stationery office was locked. Professor Bërger's well-appointed rooms, which I located in a wing upstairs with the aim of enquiring about further work, were unoccupied. I peered through the frosted glass of the double doors. He was probably on conference leave. Dr Gwin, who had proven her worth, was doubtlessly accompanying him.

Even the professor's pigeonhole in the staff room was empty, as was the staff room itself. I inserted my hand in the vacant space of the professor's pigeonhole, rubbed the worn wood and brought my hand to my nose. I thought I could smell horse manure—an odour I remembered from my childhood excursions to the racetrack—and it was then, I would say, that my lovesickness began.

I found myself at home in my one-room flat, writing lovelorn poems. On the washing machine that doubled as my desk I experimented with acrostic poems spelling out Professor Nûte Bërger—as well as the virtues of the great man—but I knew that I would never have the courage to deliver the verse into his smooth, strangely malodorous pigeonhole. Such a man, I knew, should not be forced to consider the love of one so undistinguished. I began to cry a lot, and I am ashamed to admit that I started drinking.

Then my mother came to visit. I had called her to confess that I was unemployed. She found me writing an epic, which I thought might be more to the professor's taste. The small room was carpeted with scrawled pages of verse, and I told her that I wanted to bear Professor Nûte Bërger twelve children.

My mother got me back my old job at the university creche so that I could meet the payments on my credit card, then sent me to a psychiatrist. Dr Menkowith prescribed Numpax and, without explanation, asked me to talk about my father.

Work at the creche and the Numpax prevented me from writing poetry. I began to think clearly. I knew that, in order to win the professor's affections, I needed to be more like Arda Gwin. I got a manicure and enrolled in a PhD, nominating the Bërger School of monumental poetics as my area of research. I looked through my postgraduate student email notifications

for a conference on the Bërger School. I fancied that I would give a paper and that the professor himself, having recognised my name on the programme, would watch me from a front-row auditorium seat. The conference funding, I thought, might extend to the purchase of a tidy skirt, and I would need to take out a gymnasium membership to exercise my neglected thighs.

Unfortunately—and inexplicably, given the professor's reputation—the only conference I could find on the Bërger School was the one that I had arranged the previous month. Out of desperation I turned to my haiku network conference notifications. In the process of looking through conference titles I was pleased to rediscover something of my original fascination for haiku research and my genuine longing to be part of an invigorating world of intellectual enquiry into short verse. Directly in my field of children's haiku research were Educational Haiku: A Tall Order for a Short Poem, at the University of Bulrangia, and The Forty-seventh International Conference on Teen Angst Haiku, hosted by the University of Yoon.

However, I thought of the professor and put aside my own interests. To get close to him I had to be strategic. As I did not know where he was, the best I could manage was a half-day conference hosted by the University of Lümp, near the professor's colossal poetry installations. I remembered the slides he had shown at his symposium, his polyhedral text-lettering-and-graffiti clusters magnificent beneath radioactive sediment.

The half-day conference was called In Small Doses: Feminism and Haiku. While I had little research expertise in feminism, I could quite confidently discuss the subject of haiku for young girls. I submitted an abstract and an application to my university for conference funding, with an additional request for resources to cover the purchase of protective clothing and a gas mask for my field trip to the northern suburbs of Lümp. I imagined myself inviting questions from the stage and pointing at audience members with my manicured nails, just like Dr Gwin.

It was as I was travelling to the feminist conference that my recovery began—although this was certainly not how I initially understood the violent emotions and deplorable behaviour that I exhibited during this time. On the midnight flight to Lümp, a flight attendant spilled hot coffee on my new protective pants. The man was apologetic, and in retrospect I can see that I was fortunate to be wearing such thick fabric. But at the time

I could see only that my pants had been prematurely soiled. I felt suddenly angry.

The contrite flight attendant returned to his post. I extracted a notebook and pencil from my hand luggage, and began to write—in what I can only describe as a childish frenzy—a suite of limericks ridiculing skinny men, which ended with a tirade against the stench of the racetrack. Eventually, I sedated myself with Numpax.

The flight attendant had trouble waking me upon landing at dawn, but once roused I rushed from the plane to the bus stop and, from that disintegrating and abandoned shelter, walked along the highway to the University of Lümp wearing my new gas mask. The air was thick with a brown mist that masked the remnants of the city, and I struggled to find the campus hosting the conference on feminist haiku. It was, it turned out, located underground.

Upon descending to the foyer of the arts faculty, I recalled the claustrophobic stationery office assigned to me as Professor Bërger's research assistant and was once again overcome by what I presumed at the time were hormonal waves of fury. I threw my gas mask onto the concrete floor, before recovering and fumbling in my briefcase for another Numpax. Fortunately there were no witnesses: the arts faculty was utterly deserted.

I looked at my watch and saw that I had arrived in time for the first presentation of the conference, even though I had yet to locate the venue. My paper was scheduled for before midday. According to my plans, if I left immediately following my presentation I would have enough time for my field trip to the professor's polluted poetry clusters, provided I could find a taxi willing to drive there. Then I would take another overnight flight home.

I located the conference area, a small and poorly ventilated tutorial room at the end of a labyrinthine passage, and seated myself behind nine colleagues, all of whom were already distracting themselves with portable devices of various descriptions. The presentation, a paper called 'Bite-sized: Vampire Haiku and Feminist Appetites', had begun.

I am ashamed to admit that—due to the effects of the Numpax, and perhaps my thick safety clothing and the listless air—I fell asleep, waking only for question time. When I awoke, an academic from the Open University of Ugrile in the front row was introducing himself. The fellow had self-published a chapbook of poems—copies of which, he said, indicating a suitcase at his feet, were available for sale.

The poet-academic's subsequent question to the presenter involved a lengthy and learned disquisition on the abject corpse, and its importance to soil health and plant life, to which, I must admit, I was only partially attuned. Suddenly the scholar from Ugrile uttered a name that punctured my sluggish consciousness. He referred to Zed Roānkin and his anthropological research into a uniquely grounded and utilitarian philosophy of verse.

I remembered Professor Nûte Bërger's symposium, and the cleaning woman in the audience who had asked a short and direct question about Roānkin. The professor had avoided her enquiry. I understood now that his polite smile and mobile eyebrows signalled nothing less than sheer panic. Roānkin, a dogsled driver and poetry researcher without pretensions, was his nemesis.

I left Lümp without visiting Professor Nûte Bërger's fouled poetry clusters. On the red-eye flight home that night, sleeping restlessly as a result of forgoing my customary dose of Numpax, I had various auspicious dreams. In one, the professor was mounted on a concrete racehorse that disintegrated under a hail of brown, manure-smelling sediment. In another, my mother—confused with the woman at the Bërger conference—raised a pair of birthing forceps under uncannily clear skies.

I woke, the plane having landed, with the name of Zed Roānkin on my lips. I spoke it to the dawn as I emerged onto the tarmac. I felt like a new woman. I knew what I had to do.

I went home to my bedsit, where I freshened up and burned the sheaves of verse I had composed in what I came to think of, using Dr Menkowith's term, as the period of my poetic delirium. Then I went to my mother's house, where I made breakfast for her and seven of my siblings, who remained at home under her care. I gave my mother the protective pants, which I thought she might find useful in her occupation as an animal midwife.

After that I commuted to the University of Harvikoski, where I notified the postgraduate centre of a change in my thesis topic. I would no longer be investigating the Bërger School of monumental poetry. I would instead be conducting research into fakes. Finally, I placed a note in Professor Nûte Bërger's pigeonhole in the staff room. It said: *I will expose your horseshit.* I signed it *Zed Roānkin*.

Roānkin and the Librarian

DURING MY forty-three years as a community librarian I had the misfortune to witness the pitiful withering of that body of literature known as poetry. While rumours have emerged since my retirement about my role in poetry's decline, I must insist that I was at all times professional and deeply sympathetic in my caretaking role. The truth is that I—and the now-ignominious Zed Roānkin—have been grievously misunderstood. It has been suggested that we acted maliciously against verse: that we were resentful plotters, vulgar materialists, geriatric jokers, even depraved paramours. To the last charge, let me say that my many years of handling library returns provided me with

sufficient experience of other people's bodies and their various secretions. Let me insist, too, that whatever I did to poetry, I did out of goodwill.

The problem with poetry was not that poets stopped writing. Poetry continued to be produced—just as children, in increasingly problematic numbers, continued to be born. Towards the end of my career I received notifications and order forms from poets almost daily. I continued to do my best to facilitate the passage of poetry into the world, purchasing as many publications as my meagre acquisitions budget allowed. I also received, in the daily post, self-published volumes sent by poets, both local and far-flung—books which I duly processed and included in the library's holdings.

Yet fewer and fewer readers were interested in verse. While I continued to wrap the books in protective plastic, over the years I stopped installing the expensive electromagnetic security tags. The volumes of poetry sat neglected on the steel shelves, acquiring the smell that the good patrons of the library associated with fine literature, but that I knew was mildew.

There were times when I felt as if I was working in a house of death crowded with dubiously preserved and catalogued items. There were even times when I thought of myself as akin to an angel of mercy. After closing, I would wander among the shelves like a lipsticked ghoul—I harbour no illusions about my mature appearance—withdrawing the new and pristine volumes of verse. I carried them to the loans desk and checked them out. Then I opened them, cracking their spines. Finally, I slotted the books into the returns chute, processed them at the returns desk and placed them neatly on the trolley for what I knew would be their final reshelving. At least the books, upon coming to rest and before starting to rot, would look as if they had been read.

I used also to bring the volumes home, where I would consume my meals and sometimes undertake a spot of vegetable gardening with the books open beside me. I prided myself on giving those books a sense of life, however temporary. Unfortunately, I found that I could no longer read them through. As a spinster, it was not that I lacked the time. It was that the countless volumes of lyric verse tried my patience. Although I could not eliminate age as a causative factor, poetry brought on what my blunt Cronkian ancestors knew as a *ruska rättä*. That is to say, it moved only my bowels.

I once was genuinely fond of verse. Indeed, it had inspired my professional calling, and I continued to do

my utmost to nurse poetry in its deteriorating health. True, I operated privately, which I believe fuelled the later rumours about me. I was not a member of the local poetry group, although I would like it stated for the record that I always dutifully attached their notices about readings to the library pinboard.

I knew myself, from an earlier experience, to avoid such events as one generally avoids funerals. However, I did agree to participate in one of the group's meetings, scheduled for a weekday evening, the alleged purpose of which was to devise strategies for saving poetry. How, the meeting's agenda asked, might readers be procured for the noble work of poets?

It was my feeling that readers should probably be left well enough alone. I certainly would have preferred not to be disturbed. But I had received a formal invitation from the group's chairperson, an asthmatic septuagenarian called Devereaux Disentaglio, who slyly appealed to me in my role as the community librarian. Even though I was only weeks from retirement, I knew that I was professionally obliged to attend.

I was familiar with Disentaglio as the author of *The Hallowed Ruins of the Monastery of Baptiste Bouchardon*, a self-published chapbook donated to the library eleven years ago. I remembered breaking the perfect-bound spine with great ease, before depositing the book in the returns chute. As it turned out, I was exceptionally glad to have attended Disentaglio's poetry meeting—despite much of the present malicious gossip about me later arising from that gathering. It was then, during a full-scale asthma attack by the septuagenarian poet, that I had a glimpse of how verse might truly be saved. It was then that I heard the name of Zed Roānkin.

The demise of poetry was bound up with my professional life, but it was also deeply personal. I had become enamoured of poetry in my teenage years, when I was still living in the northern land of my forebears, in the swampy and forested province of Fermine, in Cronk. While Cronkians were generally a rational people, a characteristic attributed to the emotionally anaesthetising effects of the deep snow blanketing the land for most of the year, the short months of summer made people reckless.

One summer evening I investigated the secrets of my mother's bedroom. My mother, a reindeer herder and a single parent, had been called out for an emergency. In

her absence I discovered two books of verse beneath the sensible underwear in her bedside drawer: Hilja Fănu's *The Organs of Species*, a radical volume of zoological poems, and *Farming Is Hard*, Fănu's candid pastoral work.

My mother found me engrossed in Fănu's verse when she returned from euthanising an aged reindeer whose antlers had become entangled inside a fish-drying hut. Standing at her bedroom door, stomping earth from her boots on the floorboards and scratching the mosquito bites on her sturdy calves, she agreed that I was old enough to commence the study of my nation's great and yet-untranslated body of verse.

As she returned her rifle to its case under her bed and patted her seven faithful sled dogs, all of whom had been left behind on this snowless night, she recommended a number of other poetry titles. She named Wildê Hildegaarden's *How the Mosquito Winked at Me*, a work of surprising eroticism. There were also Berthold Erkki's celebration of the endless light of the northern summer, *No Need for Electricity*, and the sober follow-up, *Restarting Your Electrical Generator*, in which Erkki switched his focus to Cronk's snowbound winters.

These books revealed to me the extraordinary and intimate facts of my world. During that youthful summer of obsessive and astonished reading, in the local marsh-encircled library, I decided to commit my life to the public custodianship of books.

Half a century later I found myself in a poorly ventilated community hall in an allegedly more civilised country. I was in the company of five local poets, who had assembled to save poetry and who had decided to commence with an impromptu reading of their own lyric verse. I consoled myself with the thought that my retirement was only weeks away.

Disentaglio took to the hall's stage, inhaled from a hand-held respiratory device and began reciting at a meticulous pace seventeen sonnets from a sequence called *The Sacred Ruins of the Castle of Pannini Pigalle*. Upon finishing his reading he announced to the audience—directing his news especially to me, I felt—that the poems were from a forthcoming self-published chapbook, which would have a limited, special-edition run of ten copies.

Evelette Krônes, whom I recognised as the secretary responsible for delivering the group's notices to the library, read next. She performed a breathless ode to the hydrangea, a plant I have always found irritatingly prone to powdery mildew. A young man with bloodshot

eyes climbed the steps to the wooden stage after her. He held some scraps of paper in his trembling hands and mumbled so badly that I found myself relieved of the obligation to make out a single line. The final reader was a middle-aged man whose suit did not appear to have been laundered for some time. By the time he had concluded his aggressive recitation of a series of limericks against his ex-wife, two hours had passed.

Only one of the five members of the writers' group had not read. This was an elderly man who was confined to a wheelchair and who seemed able to move only his eyes. On a few occasions during the reading, I thought that he might have been rolling his eyes at me. While I empathised with his plight, I was wary of making assumptions about the tics of stroke victims and carefully withheld from reciprocating.

At the end of the reading we carried our plastic chairs to a table spread with plates of tuna and pickle sandwiches, and prune and muesli cakes. Krônes fussed over the old man in the wheelchair in a way that suggested she was his carer or even his daughter. I was appalled. He had no choice, I saw, than to be here.

Krônes busied herself removing cling wrap from the plates of food, and the group of poets fell into silence and began to eat, with the exception of the old man in the wheelchair and me—possible geriatrics-in-arms, although his now-expressionless eyes across the table gave little away. There was a cask of red wine, from which the young man with the pink eyes and unfortunate tremble dispensed fluid mainly into a plastic cup.

I looked at the clock, high on the back wall of the community hall. It was already past my regular bedtime. I could just make out the tick of the clock's shuddering minute hand above the sounds of mastication and Disentaglio's wheezing.

I looked at the old man slumped in his wheelchair. He had a surprisingly dark and healthy moustache, and he reminded me of my mother, who had become vigorously hirsute in old age. My mother, still very much alive, had retired from reindeer herding at an opportune time—the industry, she said, was in sad decline—and taken up the conciliatory hobby of taxidermy. The walls and shelves of her home, as I witnessed on my last visit, were crowded with the antlered heads of the beasts she had once tended. Her home, I knew, was not dissimilar to my library.

Finally, Disentaglio put aside his tuna and pickle sandwich, inhaled from his respiratory device, and called

a start to the official business of the meeting. 'Poetry is in increasing danger of not being read,' he said, speaking as if he was still reciting one of his lyric poems.

'The task of saving the lyric poem,' he proclaimed in his measured way, 'is equivalent to that of saving civilisation. If we do nothing,' he wheezed, 'then nothing will be achieved. All that ink will have seeped into the paper for nought.' He sucked again on his inhaler and prompted his fellow poets to begin brain-storming.

The sluggish ticking of the clock and Disentaglio's light wheezing filled the silence. The middle-aged divorcee in the stained suit swallowed some prune and muesli cake. 'We could,' he offered, 'print poems on toilet paper. You know, you get a new poem each time you sit on the can and tear off a sheet.'

There were murmurs of enthusiasm from the other members of the group. I looked across the table at the old man in the wheelchair. His mouth had sagged open beneath his lush moustache.

'I think,' mumbled the young man with the bloodshot eyes, 'that it's already been done.'

When the disappointed murmurs subsided, Disen-taglio took another dose from his inhaler. 'I have my own suggestion, of course. What about,' he said, 'a poetry reading at the local library?' Disentaglio smiled, showing me his false teeth. I had been lured to the meeting under false pretences.

I spent years cultivating the polite habits of conversation favoured in my adopted country, but I am afraid to say that on this occasion I responded with regrettable candour. I informed Disentaglio that I was retiring at the end of the month and consequently was in no position to begin scheduling future events.

In retrospect, I probably should have left it there. Instead, I subjected Disentaglio and his colleagues to a disquisition on the dynamic and valuable poetry of Cronk, offering the names of key titles. I finished by providing a frank suggestion to the group about how they might help save verse. It involved them giving it up.

At this point the divorcee in the dishevelled suit began sobbing quietly. The young man looked down into the red fluid in his plastic cup. Disentaglio began sucking on his respiratory device with increasing urgency. The inhaler, it soon transpired, was empty.

Chaos descended upon the hall. Krônes rushed for a breathing apparatus, which was apparently stored

in a first-aid closet in the kitchen. The middle-aged man and the young man moved anxiously to the septuagenarian's side.

Then I noticed a surprising noise. The old man in the wheelchair across from me had closed his mouth. While his lips were unyielding beneath his bushy moustache, he seemed to be laughing.

It was probably unseemly for me to depart at such a moment. But depart I did. As I escaped through the door into the night outside, the last thing I heard was the miraculous voice of the old man in the wheelchair. It called after me—in a slurred refrain, but with increasing vigour—something that sounded like 'Zed Roānkin! Zed Roānkin!'

Perhaps I was charged with adrenaline from the dramatic unfolding of events in the community hall, but the old man's words, despite not making any sense, thrilled me.

I grant that I probably should have expressed some degree of concern for Disentaglio. The truth is, though, that I found myself utterly distracted. Regardless of the late hour, I was too excited even to return home.

I drove to the library, where I let myself in and turned on the fluorescent lights. I looked up Zed Roānkin in the catalogue. I found nothing under any of the various spellings that I investigated in the database. I went to the relevant bookshelf, but located only the volumes of mystic verse written by Roāneally and Roāquefort, their spines broken and their protective plastic covers stuck to one another on the steel shelf.

I paced along the poetry aisle, remembering the books of verse I had discovered in my mother's bedroom all those decades ago. How full of life they had been! These volumes, by contrast, seemed destined only for death.

Finally I called my mother, whom I was fortunate to catch—she was in the process of disembowelling a dead buck—but she had never heard of any poet in Cronk by the name of Zed Roānkin. She was pleased to hear that the poet's name had been associated with an old man's medical recovery, but she had a pressing obligation to a reindeer's corpse. She would have to call me back.

At that point, ensconced in my office, I succumbed to fatigue and fell asleep with my arms folded on the desk. Immediately I began dreaming. I was back at the community hall, sitting at the table spread with plates of tuna and pickle sandwiches, and prune and

muesli cakes. The four readers from the poetry group were no longer there. Sitting around the table, in the plastic chairs, were four stuffed deer. The elderly man in the wheelchair, from beneath his bushy moustache, began reciting the impromptu speech I had delivered to Disentaglio and his fellow poets. At its conclusion he stood up and cartwheeled towards the stage. Then he began laughing.

I woke up, in the hours before dawn, muttering the name of Zed Roānkin. The library was harshly lit by fluorescent lights. I knew what I had to do. I removed five pages of foolscap from my desk drawer, folded the pages in half and stapled them into an A5 booklet. Recollecting my address to the poetry group, which had provoked Disentaglio's asthma attack and the old man's astonishing revival, I wrote furiously on the pamphlet at my desk for a good hour, inspired by Cronk's materialist poetry and my mother's sled dogs. When I had finished I scrawled on the cover page the title *A Roānkin Philosophy of Poetry*. I gave the author the name of Zed Roānkin.

I could not bring myself to catalogue my subversive booklet on the poetry shelves, where I knew it would come to rest for eternity between the sticky, unwanted volumes of Roāneally and Roāquefort. Instead, I inserted it into the appropriate place in the economics section, between *Tricks to Retiring Peacefully* and *Workplace Fraud*.

There has been much speculation about my motivation in the aftermath of the pamphlet's irregular but seemingly widespread circulation and misuse. But I must insist that my motives were pure. I believed that I had discovered the secret to revitalising the dying body of verse.

Acknowledgements

Earlier versions of 'A Roānkin Philosophy of Poetry' and 'Three Sisters' were published in *Australian Book Review*. An earlier version of 'The Red Wheelbarrow' was published in *Griffith Review*, 'The Obscene Bird of Night' was published in *Westerly* and 'The Double' was published in the *Review of Australian Fiction*. I am grateful to the editors of these journals and to the staff at Text Publishing.

I would like to extend my particular appreciation to the following people: Penny Hueston, Peter Rose and Jeremy Chambers for their professional support and personal kindness; Gerald Murnane for teaching me, some twenty years ago, about precision and truth; Cassandra Atherton and Tiina Takolander for reading drafts and offering encouragement; Kate McCooey and Sam Takolander for being delightful; and Aili Takolander for her Finnish expertise and help with child minding. A special thanks to David Winter for his brilliant advice and editing; he coaxed a better book from me. Finally, my deepest thanks to David McCooey, who inspires and supports me in everything.